A Case for Line Larsen Book One:

Kari Nordmann

Lisa J Rivers

FIRST EDITION

Published in 2022 by
GREEN CAT BOOKS
19 St Christopher's Way
Pride Park
Derby
DE24 8JY

www.green-cat.shop

ISBN: 978-1-913794-04-0

CONTENTS

ACKNOWLEDGEMENTS

A BIG thank you to Karen, who was the beta reader and proofread it perfectly!

1 -Train of Thought

I flicked through my notebook several times during the train journey home. I had made some notes on this occasion, as it had been the first time I had officially taken minutes from an interview; a real-life interview, not those ones we learned about at college. The client, an unknown woman who appeared to be deaf and mute, had been accused of murder. 'Where's the victim?' I had written.

I'd have liked to return and just try and get through to this 'Kari Nordmann', as my boss had labelled her. Mr Hansen, my boss, seemed to have a clear enough conscience as he snored in the seat next to me. Luckily, I carried my trusty earphones and phone everywhere with me, so blasted out some well-chosen music that wouldn't interfere with the other passengers, or indeed my train of thought.

I couldn't understand why 'Kari' wouldn't speak, if it was indeed a choice. She just looked like a scared little girl, her large brown eyes wide in fear. Brash 'Hansen', as I called him – not to his face, obviously - had bounded his way into the room, making her flinch.

Until I started working at his law firm, I had never met anyone so obnoxious. I was hired as his legal secretary three months ago, but spent most of my days making coffee and visiting various takeaways to pick up whatever he desired to eat that day. I had been placed on a desk that was 'front-of-house', so that I could deal with whatever came through the door, or on the telephone, email; in fact, anything that he didn't have to deal with personally. That included his poor wife, Heidi, who rang him several times a day, only to be let down most days when he waved dismissively at me, saying he was too busy.

In reality, he was rarely 'too busy'. Don't get me wrong, he was a very successful lawyer, but I think that part of his success was achieved in the very early days of his law company, when he stumbled across a case where the murder trial fell apart when one of the key witnesses for the prosecution was discovered to be lying under oath. More luck than judgement, I think! So instead of Heidi chewing off his ear every day, she bothered me incessantly, telling me how proud she was of her husband. I'd never met anyone more delirious than her before either! The pair of them were at least keeping me on my toes I suppose.

I had chosen the big world of Oslo when I was little. I had always dreamed of being something quite successful, in a high building in the big city, rather than the quaint town on the outskirts of Bergen, where I was born and raised. Mamma worked away from home for a lot of the time, in Oslo of course, whilst Pappa stayed at home with us in the sleepy town, refusing to move away from his remaining family. Pappa embraced not being the main wage earner and was quite happy with his wife working away. He always said it was the secret to a happy marriage, not being underneath each other's feet all the time. 'Absence makes the heart grow fonder', he used to say. Maybe this was the key to the Hansen's marriage. Maybe if he answered her calls, the marriage would be doomed. Who knows, I just do my job!

As Kari hadn't been talkative, I didn't need to write much down, so had taken the opportunity to observe the situation instead. Hansen certainly was intimidating at the best of times, so to a shy young woman he must have been downright frightening. Words couldn't hurt her it seemed, but she flinched every time he raised his voice and jumped with every clenched fist on the table. He'd been on a course just before I started working for him, apparently; a self-assertion course, which had taught him how to be this towering inferno of a man. I chuckled to myself as I pictured his almost two-metre frame ablaze following one of his rages. His face always went a deep shade of scarlet when he was angry, which wasn't too often these days since he'd passed the majority of the 'menial' tasks to me.

I looked up from the notepad and saw that he was drooling from his open mouth. Sometimes he had that little collection of nasty white stuff at the corners of his mouth. The thought made me retch a little inside. I looked out of the window to take my mind off his grotesqueness and smiled as I saw the tall buildings of Oslo in the distance. 'Not long now', I thought as I checked my watch. We would be back at the office ten minutes before the office closed, and I wondered if I would be allowed to leave straight from the station. I lived just a short distance from the station, and it would be a welcome relief after a full day with the boss. I closed my notepad and packed it away into my small pink rucksack, retrieving my water bottle at the same time. Some of the passengers in our carriage stood up and proceeded to the doors. I now had the difficult task of waking up the sleeping ogre. I'd never travelled with him before, in fact I'd never travelled with anyone who slept during a journey. I wanted to avoid any type of physical contact with him, I hadn't been inclined to touch him, since the last time we shook hands after my interview; his cold, skinny hands had felt more like those of a skeleton, I almost felt like I had touched Death himself. I shuffled uncomfortably at this thought, accidentally tapping his shoe with my boot. He jumped and sat up swiftly, his face almost as deep as the scarlet it had been earlier.

"Ah, Larsen, I see we have reached our destination," he muttered.

He always called me by my last name, like an old schoolmaster back in the day, as Pappa used to tell us. He insisted on being addressed as Mr Hansen, 'as a mark of respect'. A lack of familiarity with him suited me fine.

"Yes, Mr Hansen. As I live so close, would it be ok if I left slightly..."

"You are paid until 16:00, Larsen, so you will work until 16:00."

I rarely *only* worked until 16:00, as he always managed to find something to add to my work pile no matter how vigilant I was at clearing my inbox, but chose not to argue. He stood up and shoved his way through the line of people who were queueing patiently. The train came to a halt, the doors opened, and he squeezed his way through.

"Come along, Larsen," he yelled back, swinging his briefcase to and fro, knocking other travellers, who muttered their displeasures to a deaf ear.

By the time I had managed to catch up with him, he had already managed to light up his cigarette and was puffing away by the entrance. Despite his apparent inability to multi-task in the office he had perfected his routine of walking, talking rubbish and retrieving a cigarette AND lighter out of his pocket at the same time. No doubt he had shoved the cigarette in his mouth ready for the second he stepped outside the building. As I approached him, I observed him sneering at people who were walking past him, silently judging them. He was no oil painting himself, with his greasy, dated hairstyle that was older than me. With no consideration for others, he walked over to the taxi rank and flicked his unfinished cigarette into the gutter. He indicated to the driver that he was ready for a ride to the office, which could have easily been walked in less time than it would take to navigate through the bustling traffic. Nevertheless, there we were, cramped into the back of a cab and zig-zagging through several lanes of traffic for optimum speed. I held onto the handle above the door, attempting to breathe the fresh air through a crack in the top of the window, detesting the smell of stale cigarette smoke which clashed with the over-used vanilla-fragranced air freshener that had been sprayed by the driver. No doubt he would do the same when we alighted.

This was the first chance at fresh air I had breathed since we met up at the station that morning. My only other opportunities today were spent standing next to him while he smoked, or sitting in a burger joint eating a burger that tasted like it had been sitting in a frying pan for most of the day. It probably had. My stomach retched involuntarily again. As soon as we arrived at the building, I opened the door and inhaled deeply.

Hansen paid the driver and waited for his change, by which time I was at the building's main entrance. I breathed in as much oxygen as my lungs could manage as he lit up another cigarette and puffed his way to the door. I rolled my eyes and entered the building, smiling at the receptionist. The building was nowhere near as sophisticated as I'd dreamed of as a girl, but Agnes, the receptionist, was an absolute star. A middle-aged woman, she had been working there since she left school. Her dark hair was greying slightly, her wrinkles were starting to appear as crow's feet and laughter lines, and laugh she did. I visited her several times a day. I was required to fetch the post every morning, which was all collated by Agnes and distributed into pigeonholes for each office to collect. The office didn't have a direct water supply, so I had to visit the kitchen whenever the coffee machine needed filling, and I made sure that this was quite regularly. Aggie and I congregated in the small communal space frequently, several times a day if I wasn't too snowed under with work.

"Good evening, Line," she greeted me, tapping her invisible watch.

I glanced at my watch. It sure was evening, five minutes after my official finishing time, and as it was Friday, I was looking forward to a few glasses of wine with my friends later.

"You missed a bit," I stated, pointing to the window.

"I can't get it any cleaner, Line," she rhymed at me.

It was a standing joke between the two of us, as she always had a cloth in her pocket to clean the windows.

"Any plans for the weekend, Aggie?" I asked and she shook her head. "You should come out with us sometime."

"*Us*?" she questioned, nodding her head at Hansen as he entered the building with his last mouthful of smoke.

I looked at him and then back at Aggie. "Nooooo! Not him!" I whispered, laughing at her facial expression.

She had the ability to make me laugh every time we saw each other. Hansen stood impatiently at the elevator door, and I pointed to the stairs. He sighed and I trotted to the stairwell. We arrived at the door at the same time, and he scrambled in his briefcase for the keys.

He only needed one key, but he had several copies of it, along with keys to the filing cabinets and anything else he could lock in the office, purely so he sounded more important when he was jangling his keys. This wasn't my assumption; this, he said, was a fact. Almost falling through the door that he had successfully managed to open, I held back until the doorway was clear. I took the notepad out of my bag and put it into the drawer, as he stood and watched, ready to lock the drawer. He never allowed anything from the office to leave the building, and that included talking about any cases, which of course I totally understood due to confidentiality.

Him hovering over me as I did it wasn't as necessary. He stood up straight when I did, put his hands on his hips, sighed proudly and announced that we could go for the weekend. We had been in the office for less than a minute. He could have easily taken the notepad up and let me leave early, or even on time, but he liked that little bit of control.

Aggie was busy gathering her belongings ready to leave when I returned to the lobby.

"Goodnight, Aggie," I said, making her jump.

"Line!" She pulled another face, which could possibly have been a genuine response to my announcement, who knows. "It will be Monday in no time,' she replied.

I laughed. "But it isn't Monday now!"

"You go and have fun, young one!" She waved me out of the door when we heard the elevator reaching the ground floor.

I scuttled out as quickly as possible, blending in with the other commuters. I'd never disliked anyone this much before, but this brutish ogre managed to push all of my buttons.

Once in my apartment, I stripped myself of the clothes I'd worn for the day and jumped straight into the shower, washing the smell of the burgers, cigarette smoke and man-sweat away. During the week, I wore the very basics of make-up and kept to my own strict dress code of shapeless trousers and thick shirts – making sure they were not see-through, of course. Now it was Friday night, and I could let my hair down a bit, literally. I opened a bottle of wine and poured myself a large glass as I got ready. Switching the cd player on to my favourite tracks, I danced around my bedroom naked. A girl should have some fun, to be sure!

I was the last of our group to arrive, the others, along with the majority of Oslo, finished early on a Friday, and the other girls gave an exaggerated cheer as I sat down. There was a glass of wine ready for me, and we clinked all of our glasses collectively to celebrate the end of another week at work. Due to the confidential nature of the clients that Hansen dealt with, I avoided all talk of work directly, but did refer to him by his first name, Kenneth, and I made sure that the girls had the correct image of him in their minds.

"Sorry I'm late, girls. Kenneth made me share a train with him today to see a client, and he snores AND drools! I had to eat at a nasty burger joint and he made me go all the way back to the office after hours just to put away my notepad."

"Does he still letch over you, Line?" Astrid asked, wrinkling up her nose in disgust.

Astrid, the blonde bombshell of our group of friends, was the shortest amongst us. She liked to be upfront about how she felt about someone, which is doubly hilarious when you see her angry, rather like a small dog yapping at your ankles. She had taken an instant dislike to Hansen since my first week at work, when I caught him trying to peer down my top. I nodded and took another large gulp of wine.

"Ugh, the revolting creep!" she shuddered. "I hope karma bites him on the ass!"

We all laughed, and I tried hard not to imagine his bony bottom. I didn't want to be put off my food. The waiter breezed over to us, looking very slick and in love with himself, and handed us the menus; we ordered another bottle of wine - this was going to be a messy night! This week's food of choice was Indian food, and the poppadoms arrived with the wine. Personally, I could have just eaten them with the delicious mango chutney and the pickles, but I always ended up with a tikka masala, as this was the only Indian dish I would eat. Pappa made it once a month to try and introduce some culture into our lives as children, but he made it less spicy than in the restaurants. Like Pappa, the girls insisted we eat here once a month too, and the waiter automatically brought us a jug of iced water, just for me.

As we tucked into our main course, Helene told us about the week's events as a graphic designer's assistant. Most of us had been at the same college together, but all studying for different careers. Helene's was art, journalism was Isabella's. Astrid had been Bella's roommate after she left college, who had bonded with us quite quickly when our weekly meetups had started.

"I spent three hours trying to explain to a client the difference between two shades of green today, he just couldn't grasp the concept that there were different shades of a colour." Helene shook her head in disappointment. "Even when I sent over a colour chart he couldn't understand, then it turned out that he was colour-blind and actually wanted orange!" We all laughed. "He sent back a picture of another company's logo and said, 'I want this green!' After that, it took all of five minutes."

"Thank goodness he wasn't one of my customers," Astrid laughed, "he would have been livid with green hair! It would have made a more interesting day though, rather than the 15 'just a trim' customers that I had." Astrid worked as a hair stylist in one of the top hairdressers in the centre, and regularly had the heads of famous people to work on, but was slightly less discreet than I was. "I did have a well-known politician in today though, it would have been great to give her hair the green look." Her blonde, curly mop of hair bounced as she laughed.

Luckily, none of us took the slightest interest in politics and Astrid could have told us it was Miss Piggy for all we knew!

I nodded to Isabella as I poured my fourth glass of water, "How about you, Tinkerbell, how was your week?"

We always called Isabella Tinkerbell, she was obsessed with the Disney character for a while and regularly wore green.

"It was ok," she replied.

"Is that it?" Astrid responded, a quizzical look on her face.

Belle shrugged and swallowed her mouthful of rogan josh. "Nothing much has happened in the coffee-making department of

Oslo's most famous magazine, 'The Fishermen's Monthly'! Although, Bjørn Sorensen caught a large fish of some sort last weekend!" she laughed, shovelling another mouthful of food into her mouth.

"Something better will come along soon, Tinkerbella, don't give up hope, eh?" I comforted. "I'm the coffeemaker in our office too, remember? At least your boss isn't a perv!"

"I think I would be grateful for the attention actually," Isabella replied, a cheeky little smile forming at the corner of her mouth.

We all knew that she had a major crush on her boss, which was why she chose The Fishermen's Monthly as her workplace. It came as a grave disappointment when she discovered that her colleague, Linn, was Fredrik's girlfriend.

"You can have my stalker if you prefer," I offered sarcastically.

She shook her head fiercely and we all laughed. We finished the rest of the wine, paid the waiter, and headed for the cold outdoors. I wrapped my coat around me tightly as the icy wind hit us. I grappled for my hat which I had tucked into the pocket, and Astrid laughed.

"It'll mess your hair up, Line, leave the hat."

"That's great coming from someone who is too short to feel the bitter air up here!" I teased. "Don't be a kid, Astrid."

"I'll make your hair greener, Line," she rhymed back at me, grinning.

***

The rest of Friday night, along with most of Saturday was just a blur to me, thanks to the excessive mixing of drinks at the club we had ventured to. I woke up mid-afternoon on the Saturday, to a clattering sound and the smell of coffee. I rolled out of bed and stumbled into the tiny kitchen/diner section of my apartment. It was Isabella.

"Hey, Tinkerbella, what are you doing here?" I enquired hoarsely, slumping into my favourite chair. My head was thumping, and she wandered over to me with a cup of coffee and some painkillers.

"You don't remember inviting us, and half of the club, over to your place last night?" she replied, laughing. I shook my head and frowned. "Don't worry, it was just me and Astrid here, we managed to slip out of the other entrance by the toilets without attracting the attention of all of the men you invited." I looked around. "Astrid left for work ages ago. Helene went round to Petter's place in an Uber."

My mouth was too dry to respond so I just smiled weakly, swallowed the tablets with some coffee, pulled the fluffy pink blanket that was draped over the chair around me and closed my eyes.

***

The next time I woke the apartment was dark and empty. With the blanket still around me, I manoeuvred around the abandoned items of clothing and into the bathroom for a much-needed shower. Feeling a bit more human, I made a fresh pot of coffee and peered into the fridge to see if there was anything to eat. All I could see was a microwavable burger, which reminded me of the burger I had eaten the previous day with Hansen, so I promptly shut the fridge door and vomited in the sink.

***

Sunday was a lovely long and refreshing day, with no sign of a hangover. It was unfortunate that I have a low tolerance to alcohol, and it was clear that I had attempted to keep up with the others. Bad mistake, one that shall never be repeated, I told myself. I showered (again) and rather than head for the fridge, I left the apartment in search of food. My preferred coffee shop had a few spare seats, so I stepped inside and ordered a coffee and toast. There was a newspaper on the table, left by the previous occupants, so I picked it up and inspected it.

"Hey, Line," a voice spoke.

As I looked up, I felt my face flush. It was Thorfinn, the guy I had been in love with since school. He didn't know it of course! Secret crushes were my thing so far in life!

"Hey, Thor," I replied, a little later than expected, thanks to my screaming inner monologue. "What are you doing in Oslo?"

"I moved here a few months ago to get married." The words hit me like a brick to the head. Had I been drinking my coffee I would have spat it out and probably had one of my famous choking fits that always make my friends laugh. Instead, I smiled without warmth and congratulated him. Hoping that he would move onto whatever hell he had come from, he sat down in the chair opposite me. As much as I wanted to leave, I was transfixed by his deep-blue eyes. Words failed me, and I prayed that he'd break the silence by either speaking or leaving. This was the first time I'd wanted him to leave, I usually attempted to summon up a superpower to get him to be this close to me.

I realised that he wasn't going to speak, and that I was staring at him. "I...I..I've only been here a few months too. You'll have to show me the sights someday," I blurted.

Why would he give me a sightseeing tour, and why was I flirting with a married man? I'd had years to flirt with him but had been too shy to. He smiled at me with those brilliant-white teeth, and I felt the twang of my heart as he did so.

"I'll hold you to that," he teased.

"You'd better," I replied, winking an eye and gesturing with a finger like a smoking gun. Stupid!

The waiter arrived with my toast and Thor's takeaway bag.

"Is that a Sunday brunch treat for the wife?" Why was I engaging with him about his wife? I was probably giving him ideas to make his marriage even stronger than it ever was.

"No. It's for me, selfish pig, eh?! I have to go though, I have a soccer match to get to!"

I looked at him, for his soccer kit, but he was wearing jeans and hiking boots. "No, it's not me playing, just a spectator," he replied to my silent question.

He lingered, for as long as I used to at school, then smiled and said goodbye. I watched him leave, watched his ass leave to be more precise. Shaking, I retrieved my phone out of my coat pocket and sent a text to my sister, Lillianne, telling her everything. She rang me within minutes. She always rang whether I preferred to communicate by text message or not.

"...And you let him leave? Do you even have a way to contact him?" she started the conversation.

"He's married, Lilli, it's too late for me. Pipped to the post by Mrs frikkin' Valle, sis. All those years of admiration wasted. Thorfinn Valle will never be mine."

There was a cough behind me, and Thor reached over. "I forgot my scarf," he announced. "Oh, and if you need any crime-fighting doing, give me a bell," he added, passing me a business card.

He smiled, winked and left again. I couldn't speak. Lilli had gone quiet too, then I realised she was pausing for breath before laughing loudly. She had heard too! I had no words, so I just made my excuses and ended the call.

2 – Afternoon High

Monday came around too soon, as it always seems to. I had spent the remainder of Sunday hiking a nearby national park to clear my thoughts, detoxing my body of the poor weekend choices, wallowing in my little love/hate bubble. Loved that I had seen Thor again, hated that he was now married. I'd attempted a super-sleuth marathon of trying to find where he and his wife lived and if she was known around Oslo, and his business card was well-worn from where I had held it until it was crumpled. So far, my efforts had failed, and now here I was, walking the short distance to the office for another week of coffee-making and phone-answering.

It was getting colder every day, not surprising as we were getting closer to winter every day! I had allowed myself to get to the office a little early, to give me time to sort out my hair once I removed my woolly hat, and Aggie was mooching around the reception when I arrived. She smiled when I tapped on the door and she came to open it, still carrying her watering can.

"Good morning, Aggie," I greeted her. "Is it so cold that you are having to oil your joints?" I asked, nodding at the watering can.

She looked at me, frowned and then laughed, pulling one of her hilarious faces. "You are such a tease, Line. It is so that I can water the plants."

Aggie was funny. I wasn't sure if she had a slight learning disorder or thought that I did, but she often over-explained things and didn't always understand my humour. Bless her though, she was lovely. She was busy pottering around the kitchen making us both a coffee whilst I was tidying my hair in the mirror of the cloakroom. I hung my coat up and we met at the wall between the two rooms, almost bumping into each other.

"Coffee, Line?" she said, shoving the mug of sweet, hot, brown liquid in my hand.

It smelled divine. I sat at the little kitchen table and held the mug in both hands to warm them up. She sat next to me, and we chatted about our weekends. Aggie lived with her husband, Anders, and had two adult sons who were both living away from home. She was hoping to be 'blessed' with grandchildren, and it made me wonder whether I was the abnormal one for not desiring children, let alone grandchildren. Aggie was already married and a mother at my age; it seemed strange to me. I suppose it was a different time back then.

My phone alarm started playing the 'death tune' as I called it, indicating that I had a minute to get upstairs in time for work, so I drained my cup and grabbed the coffee pot filled with water, and bid my farewell to Aggie. She pottered to the front doors as slowly as possible, making Hansen wait for it to be unlocked. The colder the weather was, the slower she would be, blaming it on her arthritis. We all have our little joys in life, and we both disliked Hansen equally.

I was waiting at the office door when he finally emerged from the lift, wheezing from the cold, tobacco and the slight walk all rolled into one. Scrambling in his pointless brown briefcase he found his massive set of keys, taking ages to sort through to find the one for the office door - which most of them were - as was his first daily ritual upon arriving. He pushed his way through the door, not holding it for me despite the juggling of my bag, the coffee pot and our mugs, but this was not unusual either. I set the coffee pot down with the mugs and filled the machine with coffee from the cupboard, once Hansen had unlocked it. It started gurgling and the beautiful aroma filled the air instantly.

My second job of the day was to fetch pastries for Mr 'never puts on weight' Hansen, which meant I had to leave almost as soon as I arrived. When I first started working here, I would bring the pastries with me before I started work, but I soon wised up to that, realising that I could make it part of my working hours rather than during my own time. He kept me there long enough as it was, so all food runs now formed part of the working day. I loitered around him, waiting for the petty cash box to be unlocked; pastries were classed as a work expense apparently.

He handed me a 100 kroner note. "Don't forget the receipt," he reminded me.

He reminded me every day, and I had provided a receipt every day, except the first day when I didn't know I had to and as a result he had not recompensed me, so I had essentially paid for his first pastries. I had made a point of asking for a receipt from then on, explaining to the coffee shop owner, Marit, why I needed it, and from then on she had hiked the price up and popped an extra pastry in a separate wrapper for me, marking the receipt as 'miscellaneous pastries'. I grabbed my hat and coat from the cloakroom and wrapped my scarf tightly around the gap between my coat and hat. It may only be a short walk to the coffee shop, but I wasn't getting frostbite for Hansen!

"Cake!" Aggie laughed as I walked past her, as she did every day.

Day to day work life was essentially the same for me, yet I detested routine and habits. Turn left out of the building, walk 35 steps, turn left into coffee shop. Every day! Marit had the box prepped and ready to go by the time I reached the counter, and she was just waiting for me to choose what I wanted to complete the transaction. What an exciting life I led! Back at the office (turn right out of coffee shop, walk 35 steps and turn right into building. Walk past Aggie. "Post is here," she says, and I smile and nod. Walk straight to kitchen and put my pastry in the cupboard, hang coat and hat up in the cloakroom, turn right out of the cloakroom towards the stairs. Walk up one flight, turn left into corridor and left into office. Walk into Hansen's office and hand him his pastries and the receipt and change. Hansen checks change and puts both in the petty cash box, locking it and storing in his drawer). Every day!

I grabbed myself a coffee and sat at my desk, switching on my computer ready to load up the emails. I looked up at the clock. It was 09.30, as it always was once this stage was completed. I sipped at my coffee as the emails loaded up. There was rarely much excitement in that department either. Hansen essentially gained the majority of his work as referrals from the state, for those clients who didn't have a lawyer. He rarely won any of these cases as they were 'open and shut guilty clients' as he worded it. He still got paid, but allowed them to slide from his portfolio. He happily took the money for the little work he needed to do, deciding that they were guilty before making first contact. From what I had heard through the grapevine (Aggie) he visited the client three times; once in the police station of the arrest, once in the holding jail and then the next time he saw them was for a quick de-brief an hour before court started. I hadn't been invited to the first visit for Kari, as it involved a plane flight and that was too expensive for Hansen. Money was higher up on his list of priorities than reputation, although that was a close second place. Well, he had completed his first two meetings with Kari, so we were just to wait for the court date, and check if there were any more clients.

No emails.

Next on the daily chores list was to go back downstairs and retrieve the mail from Aggie. I shut my rucksack in my drawer and locked it. Downing my coffee, I told Hansen where I was going and escaped, casually walking down the stairs at my own speed. The only mail we had was a few leaflets and an invoice for the use of the office, which Aggie was just placing in the envelope when I reached her desk.

"Ooohh, Mr H won't be pleased with that, Aggie," I said, knowing how elusive Hansen became when he had to pay rent for his office.

She smiled and handed the envelope to me. "No doubt he will suddenly have a VIP case somewhere far away," Aggie agreed.

"I can hope!" I laughed.

When I returned to the office, Hansen was hovering around my desk. I was glad that I had my bag safe at all times, otherwise he would probably be rifling through it whenever I left the room.

"Just one letter for you today, Mr Hansen," I smiled at him and handed over the letter with inner satisfaction.

He disappeared into his office and then returned with a flimsy A4 file with '*NORDMANN: K #14 – CONFIDENTIAL*' written on it.

"Your work for the rest of the week, Larsen. We will be called to court soon on this case and I need you to sort the brief out."

Sort the brief out? I'd been trained to write minutes and notes, and knew some legal jargon but it was the responsibility of the lawyer to write the brief, or so I'd been told. I looked at him blankly. He sighed and stuck his hand in his pocket, leaning over my desk until his head was almost buried in my chest. I pushed my chair away using my boot to kick the floor in disgust, and he waved a key at me, opening my drawer with the notepad in.

"Here," he said, passing me the book, "use your notes."

"But, Mr Hansen, the client didn't say anything, so I had nothing to write down."

"Well, in the file you will find the initial report and notes from the custodial unit. Just copy that out and add the notes that the client was 'unwilling to co-operate'."

At that, he strode casually back into his office, closing his door and opening his window, lighting up a cigarette. He knew it was illegal to smoke in the building, so he was always prepared to use his law jargon to say that 'technically he wasn't smoking *in* the building'.

I opened the file and pulled out three pieces of paper. One was, indeed, the initial report from when the 'alleged witness' rang the emergency services claiming that a woman had killed someone. The second, the custodial report stated that the murder suspect had remained at the location waiting to be picked up by the authorities, but was unwilling to co-operate in the search for the victim, and had not spoken since that day. There was slip of paper attached to this with a paperclip to show that Hansen had attempted to interview her then, but no luck. 'So this automatically means that the suspect is guilty then?' I said to myself, shaking my head in disbelief. The third piece of paper was a blank template for me to complete and send to the judge ahead of the case. I looked closer at the paper and found that Hansen has circled 'GUILTY PLEA'. She had already been advised to plead guilty to avoid a lengthy trial. Next to it, the client's signature had a strikethrough and 'refused to sign' had replaced the signature. Hansen clearly didn't have a conscience, which some would say was a prerequisite of becoming a lawyer, but I did. I couldn't let this young woman be sent to prison for a large chunk of her life, purely due to a lazy defence counsel.

The waft of cigarette smoke distracted me from the template and Hansen was standing at the desk, clearing his throat to get my attention.

"We're out of coffee, Larsen," he announced. "If you aren't going to keep it topped up responsibly then we are going to have to discuss you purchasing your beverages elsewhere, aren't we?"

This was the first time in three months that I had let the coffee machine go dry, and had only consumed one cup so far today anyway. 'Fine by me, Hansen', I thought, as I smiled and walked over to the machine to collect the glass jug. 'I'd happily smash this over your head, Hansen,' my inner monologue continued as I strolled out of the office. I refused to let him see when I was angry, as it seemed like he'd revel in me being angry, and I didn't want to give him the satisfaction. By the time I reached the kitchen, I was muttering obscenities to myself.

"You're a bit late for the coffee, aren't you?" Aggie announced, startling me.

There was no malice, no bad intentions to her statement.

"Took my eye off the ball, didn't I?" I replied, tutting and shaking my head in mock remorse.

"Having a bad day?"

"No, just been given some new work that I'm struggling to understand. It's a pity everything is confidential, as I have no one except Hansen to ask."

"How about your last college tutor?" she suggested.

"Ah! Good idea, Aggie!" I gave her a hug and returned upstairs with the jug of water.

Glancing at the clock whilst I was refilling the coffee machine, I saw that it was 11:00, time for me to pop out and get Hansen's lunch, and then have lunch myself. This would be an ideal opportunity for me to contact my former tutor, Ingrid, as she would be in between lessons then too. I grabbed my bag and popped my head into Hansen's office.

"Lunch?" I asked cheerily.

He looked at his watch and raised his eyebrows. "The usual,

Larsen." He opened up his petty cash box and handed me a couple of 100 kroner notes.

A trip to McDonalds it was then. I skipped happily downstairs and grabbed my coat and hat, waving to Aggie who was eating a sandwich behind her desk. Once outside, I pulled out my phone from my bag and scrolled down the contacts list until I found Ingrid's name. It connected quickly and she answered immediately.

"Ingrid? It's Line Larsen, from your class last year," I started. "I have a little query I'd like to chat to you about, if possible?"

"LINE!" she responded. "Sure, I'm marking some papers right now, but we can meet after work if you would like?"

I wasn't fond of phone calls anyway, so we arranged to meet at our usual coffee shop just off the college campus at 16:30. I continued on my way to get Hansen's two burgers with fries. Hansen was on the phone when I returned, pacing the floor like he did for most of the day, but this time with his office door shut, so I left his food on my desk with the receipt and change and ventured back downstairs for my lunch in the kitchen. I had opted for a salmon and cream cheese sandwich today, made and wrapped last night, and ate it slowly, savouring every mouthful and every second of my 30-minute lunch break. I decided to save the pastry until my last trip to the kitchen before the end of work, so that I wasn't too hungry on the way to meet Ingrid. However, I did decide to treat myself to a hot chocolate which I would ensure smelled delicious in the office, to rub Hansen's nose in it after the coffee 'fiasco' earlier. Feeling pleased with my decision, I again grabbed my coat and hat and ventured to the coffee shop and grabbed the largest, sweetest, creamiest hot chocolate that they sold.

The usual daily routine of life in Hansen's office continued with two trips to fill up the coffee pot, two phone calls from Heidi and no emails. I looked at the briefing template again whilst sipping my beverage and started to complete it in pencil, for now, focusing on the basic details. Even the basic of basic details were difficult as we knew nothing about the client, not even her name or address. Hoping for some answers later with Ingrid, I gathered my belongings and stared at the clock. As soon as 16:00 appeared I was off, before Hansen had a chance to stop me, grabbing my pastry and coat on the way.

It was a longer walk to college than my apartment, but the journey was pleasant, the pastry was delicious, and I was feeling positive about meeting up with Ingrid. It had been a few months since I had seen her, and we had always had a good rapport. The campus coffee shop was quite busy, but I caught sight of Ingrid sitting at the back with her laptop and walked over to join her. She stood up to greet me, embracing me warmly. I removed my attire and sat down opposite her.

"I always manage to get a seat in here," she smiled, "I'm a regular! I have ordered a coffee pot for two, help yourself." I thanked her and poured some into a cup. "So, how can I help you, Line?"

I took a sip of the hot coffee and replied. "I managed to get a job working at a law firm, as a legal secretary, and the owner is a bit of a lazy idiot, to be brutally honest."

Ingrid nodded, "The higher up they are, the more stupid and lazy they become!"

"Present company excepted," I added.

"Indeed, although I have taken steps away from stupidity by teaching rather than practising."

I nodded and continued. "Due to confidentiality, of course, I can't divulge too much information but knew my best idea would be to ask your advice. He has given me a template form for a guilty plea, which I need to complete to form the brief, to be handed to the judge, but we didn't learn about it."

"Ok," Ingrid replied between sips, "so you need me to help you complete the form, to show you how to do it for future use?"

"Yes, I guess, but... well, this one is a bit more complicated. The accused appears to be deaf and mute. She won't give us any of her details, verbally or written."

"Hmmm, so what evidence does this lawyer have, to make her plead guilty?"

"Nothing. We visited her last week for about an hour or so, but as she didn't speak or respond at all we only have the evidence provided by the custodial system. The thing is.... she's been accused of quite a bad crime, but there's no evidence of this crime, not even a victim."

"So then you need to find evidence, I would think," Ingrid suggested.

"My boss won't investigate it any further. He'd rather have the payment for continuing with the case until conviction rather than collect a higher reward for getting her acquitted."

"So, he doesn't care about his reputation?" Ingrid seemed confused.

"Not that I can tell. He seems more interested in a paycheque."

"Kenneth Hansen!" Ingrid announced.

"Huh?" I replied, feigning vagueness.

"I know, you can't say who it is, but I have heard through the grapevine about him in the past. He won that case a few years back, didn't he? Oh yes, sorry, I'm not asking you, it was rhetorical. It's good for his wallet but not good for justice."

"Exactly. I feel my hands are tied, but I want to help her. I want a clear conscience too, rather than just send her to prison without a chance."

"Hmmmm, let me think."

We sat in silence, and I could almost hear the cogs turning in her head. She did this a lot in class too. The first time she did it, I thought she was having a seizure. I soon learned the signs: looking into the distance, tapping the pen on her teeth, grabbing the relevant book from her bookshelf and leafing through it until she found the right solution. Another pot of coffee arrived, and I poured us both a fresh cup. I could feel the barista still hovering, so I passed him the empty coffee pot. Looking up, I discovered that it wasn't the barista, it was Thor!

"Hi, Line, I see Ingrid is deep in thought." We both looked over to see her tapping her teeth with her pen, staring at a picture of a coffee bean on the wall. "What are you doing here, Line? Stalking me?"

"I was a student of Ingrid's last year," I explained. "You?"

Thor dragged a chair over to our table and joined us. "A current law student."

"Oh, I thought you were here to get married?"

"Getting married isn't an occupation, Line, I'm a junior lawyer nearby, and have law classes here in the evenings."

I didn't have a response for him, and we were in danger of another awkward silence, until Ingrid re-joined us.

"Ah, Thor!" We both jumped. "I see you have met Line. She has a predicament that I'm trying to advise her about."

Thor turned to me and smiled. "What's the problem, Line?"

I loved the way he said my name. He had said it more times in the last couple of days than the whole time we'd attended school. Focus, Line! Before I had the opportunity to reply, Ingrid spoke up again.

"She has a client that she has to present a defence brief for, but the accused isn't very responsive. Would you think it's a sign that she is guilty, Thor?"

"Is she aggressively silent?" he asked, and they both turned to look at me.

"Erm, no, it's almost as if she is deaf and mute. That was my first impression of her. I was with her for an hour or so and she made no effort to defend herself."

"Was, erm, 'your boss' asking the right questions?" Ingrid enquired, being careful not to divulge too much confidential information.

"He wasn't really asking anything relevant except to ask why she did the crime, and banged his fist on the table a lot."

"Sounds like a great lawyer to be inspired by," Thor remarked sarcastically, and Ingrid nodded.

"Did she react to that behaviour?" Thor questioned.

"Yes, she flinched quite a bit."

"Well she couldn't be deaf then, surely?" Thor reasoned.

"She could have been responding to the vibrations or the gestures," Ingrid suggested. "Ok, firstly, see how long the deadline is to submit the plea, to see how much time you have to give this a try. If you have time, fill the form out as much as possible and see what information you need to complete it. I'm sure your boss won't mind you taking the initiative as long as it doesn't break the confidentiality, you do the other work for him too and it doesn't cost him any extra money. How does that sound?" I nodded, not quite knowing where to start. "Personally, I would start with the custodial and emergency services. See if you can get a recording of the initial emergency phone call and see if there's any more evidence that has been found since the initial reports were written."

"That sounds like a good plan, Ingrid, thank you so much!"

"Keep me informed, Line, I'll be interested to see how this develops. Now, Thor, let's get over to the classroom and get started with your work."

Thor nodded and stood up.

"Don't forget your scarf, Thor," I laughed.

***

The next day my walk to work was far more enjoyable. Just knowing that I could do more than coffee and food runs made me as excited as my first day there. It was like a breath of fresh air, a new lease of life. Not only had I had yet another conversation with Thor, but I had a chance to prove myself to Hansen, and possibly even earn him a bit of extra money, which he might pass some on to me too as a bonus. Ok, so the bonus was probably unlikely, but the rest was still positive.

Once I had completed the first routines of the day; the coffee pot, pastries, emails and mail, I was ready to get started. To begin with, I photocopied the original documents and put them into a different pile. I looked at the original brief document and completed all that I could, which was basically the date and time of arrest, arresting officer and what Kari had been charged with: MURDER. I found that I had four weeks to submit this, so set a reminder on my computer calendar. Hansen came out briefly for a coffee then returned to his office and closed the door behind him. GREAT! I took out the paper detailing the emergency call and found the number to call. I double checked that Hansen was busy, lifted the receiver and dialled the number. A lady answered.

"Hello. Please could I speak to the person who I can obtain a recording of an emergency call from?" I asked politely.

"Who is calling?"

I became nervous that they would refuse or even report me to Hansen. "My name is Line Larsen, and I work with Kenneth Hansen, at 'Hansen and Associates'." That was funny, as he didn't have any associates!

"One moment."

My mouth was dry from nerves, so I had to take a sip of coffee before continuing the call.

"Hello?" I was speaking to the same person again, my heart dropped slightly. "If you send us an email with the details, we can forward the mp3 file. The email address is on the report."

"Oh, thank you very much, have a nice day!"

I immediately emailed them and eagerly waited a response.

I tried to keep myself busy for the rest of the day, as sitting in front of a pc all day would make the day go too slowly. I refreshed the coffee, fetched the lunch, ate the secret pastry and drank the indulgent hot chocolate that was to become the new norm.

Every spare moment was spent refreshing my emails, until Hansen emerged from his office looking flustered at around 15:00 and spent the remainder of the day pacing round the whole office drinking coffee. He was eager to leave on time today, and just as I was logging out of the emails tab a new message appeared. Typical.

That would have to wait until tomorrow.

3 – The Swing of Things

I was chomping at the bit the next day and arrived at work before Agnes. I found myself pacing like Hansen; that would need to be 'nipped in the bud', I really didn't want him as a role model for my behaviour! I popped round to Marit's for a coffee to keep me warm and by the time I got back, Aggie was unlocking the door to the office. She turned round to close the door and jumped when she saw me.

"My, my, you are an early bird this morning!"

"Yes, I have an exciting day of work planned," I replied.

"Well, you can't get started until Mr Hansen gets here, you know."

"I know, I just couldn't sleep well. I had a great little catch up with my tutor, Ingrid, and she has given me a few ideas which could help this case we're working on."

"We?" Aggie questioned.

I pulled a face. "Well, I suppose it's more *me*."

She nodded. "Hmmmm, that sounds more like it!"

I sat down on one of the comfy chairs in the reception area and sipped my coffee. I'd probably be better suited to easing off the caffeine a bit, if it was making me this ... alert! Aggie busied herself dusting the furniture and clattering around in the kitchen as I waited for Hansen to turn up. At 07:59 my alarm rang, and I eased myself out of the chair that had moulded around me and hung up my things in the cloakroom.

"Have a productive day, Line," Aggie shouted as I trotted up the stairs.

Coffee pot. Pastries. Mail. Coffee. Lunch run. Coffee. Time to settle down and get my work done.

The computer seemed to take forever to load up the email page, so I grabbed myself a coffee to pass the time away. As I returned to my seat, I could see that I had an email. I scooted on my chair over to the machine and clicked the email. It was the mp3 recording that I had been waiting for. Now I had to wait for Hansen to have one of his 'very important' phone calls so that I could listen to it.

Unfortunately, this never happened, and I felt defeated. I unlocked my desk drawer and pulled my bag out. My phone fell out of the front pocket and as I bent over to pick it up, I saw that I had an email from Mamma. I clicked the message and saw that she had invited me for lunch this weekend. No doubt she would want to come round to my apartment and figured I would have to tidy up a bit. I suppose it would keep my mind off work. It was then that I realised I could forward the email from the emergency services through to my personal email address and listen to it on my phone. Genius! This task was completed with minimum fuss or attention, and I slipped my phone back into my bag as I closed down the computer. We both left the office at the same time, although I didn't wait for Hansen to lock up.

I couldn't wait till I got home, so I plugged my earphones into my phone and listened to the mp3 recording on the way home.

"Hello? Please help. I've just seen somebody come out of the forest with blood all over her. I think she has killed someone."

"Ok, miss, stay calm. What is your name? Do you feel like you are in danger too?"

"No, I don't want to give my name. Come quick."

"Ok, where is the exact location please?"

....

“Hello. Are you still there?”

I had listened to it 14 times on the short walk home. As soon as I walked into my apartment, I kicked my boots off, removed my earphones, untied my scarf and threw it, with my coat, on the back of the door. A day without lunch meant that I was extra hungry, so I threw some pasta into a saucepan, grabbed my notebook from the counter and sat down on the kitchen stool ready to take notes. I hadn't thought to check where Kari had been found, and the caller had said that it was a forest. Norway certainly isn't short of forests, that I was sure of. I made a note to check which forest it was on the reports in the morning. Kari has been seen covered in blood; was it the 'victim's', or her blood? Was that even Kari? It could have been Kari that was brought into the police station, but could it have been someone else that the witness saw? It could have been Kari who was the victim? I wrote all of this in my notebook and attended to my pasta before it boiled dry, adding a generous spoonful of pesto and mixing it through.

With a full stomach and a glass of wine, I retired to my chair, put my earphones on and listened to the call recording a few more times until sleep overcame me.

***

When I awoke it was still dark. I checked my phone for the time, but the battery had died. I reached over to my side table and switched the lamp on. I spooned some coffee into my little cafetière and switched the kettle on. Once boiled, I poured in enough water and left it to brew. My phone charger was in my bedroom, so I sleepily stumbled there and plugged the phone in. I lay on my bed, waiting for a sign of life and the phone responded quickly. It was 06:48, so I stripped out of yesterday's clothes and threw them in the hamper, along with a few other items that hadn't quite reached it this week. I caught a couple of flashes of lightning from the mirror's reflection; I loved storms. I quickly showered and dressed, hoping to catch it, but by the time I was ready there was no sign of any storm, not even rain.

I ventured into the kitchen and washed last night's dinner plate, cutlery and my wine glass. I reached into the cupboard for my green bamboo travel mug, pushed down the plunger on the cafetière and poured the coffee in. I decided to wear my yellow raincoat, just in case the rain appeared on my way to or from work. Grabbing my phone, earphones and notebook, I shoved them all into my bag and began my daily journey.

I arrived at work right on time, and the main doors were already unlocked. I hung up my dry raincoat, grabbed the coffee pot already filled with water, and hummed all the way upstairs. Hansen hadn't arrived yet, so I slid to the floor to sit and wait for him, retrieving my phone and earphones out of my bag to listen to the mp3 recording again. I had managed to listen to it three times before Hansen arrived and unlocked the door.

I headed straight to the coffee machine and switched it on. Hansen was already pacing the floor on his mobile phone and seemed rather agitated. I took this opportunity and listened to the message once more time, writing the information into my notebook. This notebook wasn't the one I used for work, so I had to ensure that I kept it separate, otherwise I risked Hansen reading it unnecessarily. I slipped it back into my bag and locked it away, along with my phone and earphones. The morning dragged, not helped by Hansen looming over me between calls.

Pastries, mail and lunch out of the way, I devoted some time to the case at last. I couldn't listen to the recording because Hansen maintained a constant presence within the office all day, but I had managed to write down some notes in my notebook. Sneaking a look, I transferred the information onto scraps of paper, using my best skill so far - shorthand. I may not know all the answers when it comes to legal knowledge, but I knew that Hansen didn't know the first thing about shorthand. I remember during my interview for this job, I was asked into a small mock meeting, quite random as it was only Hansen in the meeting. He reeled off many long legal words and spoke swiftly to try and 'catch me out'. He stood up, as he found the momentum was more professional, although I'm sure that this had the adverse effect in a regular meeting scenario. At one point he had looked over my shoulder and I knew then that I shouldn't have worn a loose blouse, as I was sure he was looking down my top. I unconsciously pulled the blouse where it was gaping, and he retreated slightly. He turned his gaze towards my notebook and remarked that 'if you are bored with the meeting, then it might be advisable to not continue with the interview procedure, and it is highly unprofessional to be doodling at this time'. It was at that point that I reeled off everything he had said, word perfect. Using this to my advantage, I had explained that the 'doodling' was a way of making me more productive, and he had bought the story. This had come in handy many times since I started working.

I positioned myself at my desk as if I were working on the computer, despite Hansen rarely giving me any work to do, and refreshed my emails every few minutes. In the remaining time, I looked at my notes, and added some fresh ideas.

How had the immediate responders known that it was Kari who had committed a murder?

Could Kari have been the victim of an assault, rather than the abuser?

No body, or other injured person, has been discovered yet.

I sat and thought, clicking refresh on my emails again. 'What if there *was* an 'injured' person?', I thought.

What if the caller was the injured person, or even the abuser? I wrote. *Were there any injuries on Kari?*

I retrieved the custodial report from the flimsy folder. 'Picked up from the road by the side of the forest, where suspect was waiting', it read.

If someone had been guilty of such a serious offence as murder, would they stay in the place where they had been spotted by witnesses?

I pondered this whilst I refilled the coffee pot, ensuring that I hid the notepad before leaving my desk. 'No, a suspect would either attack the witnesses too, depending on the circumstances of the crime, or run off and attempt to disappear', I deduced, writing that down upon my return. There seemed to be a discrepancy amongst the files in the folder; The precise location of the pickup was unknown, in fact not even the forest had been confirmed. There was no precise time of pickup, which in turn couldn't be compared to the time of the emergency call. I added these to my notebook, along with a reminder to ask the police station if any further investigations had taken place to find a body in the forest, or indeed a weapon. I checked the telephone number for the immediate responders and the custodial staff on the internet and wrote them down next to the relevant questions. 'Would I have time to call them today?', I thought. I looked at the time on the screen; 15.48. Hansen had been mooching around the office all afternoon, so I cleaned up the office and prepared for the end of the workday.

After work, I stayed and chatted to Aggie for a short while; I felt that I had neglected her slightly today as I had rarely seen her.

"Did you see the lightning this morning?" I asked her. "I was hoping for a storm but was out of luck, it seems."

"I didn't see any, Line, maybe it was only on this side of town."

Agnes lived in what she described as the 'poorer' end of town, and was so ashamed of the location that she refused say where it was, never mind invite people round to visit. She had been married quite young and children followed closely after the wedding, so as a result her and her husband had not been able to buy a house too close to Oslo. She had been a housewife until the children left home, with just this 'little job', as my mamma would say. Apart from that, they had lived on just a janitor's wage. I had grown up in similar circumstances but had the luck of a parent working a very well-paid job, along with a nice house inherited by my pappa. Aggie never grumbled about her background or current circumstances; she had been happily married for around 30 years so far, which was fairly impressive. She had two sons, and it seemed that I was slowly becoming her only daughter. She often talked about her family with immense pride. She was more than content with the outcome and had no regrets. To have two role models, Aggie and my mamma, with such similar but diverse circumstances filled me with aspiration. I had loved Thor from afar for so many years, but to have a career I loved along with a boyfriend was my dream.

I had ensured that I had brought my notebook home with me, and as I ate my dinner, I read through my notes again.

How did the witness know Kari had killed someone? Sure, they said she was covered in blood, but she may have fallen in the forest and cut herself. Had they seen her go into the forest with someone else, only to return alone, or were they just assuming?

So much of this case didn't make sense, and I soon realised that I was assuming that Kari was innocent as much as Hansen assumed she was guilty. Maybe I should just stick to my work and not dabble. BUT it didn't make sense, and I couldn't just let it lie. This poor young woman faced a lifetime in prison for a crime that not only had she possibly not committed, but may have not even taken place. My brain was too full of unanswered questions, and I knew I couldn't keep obsessing over this case as there wouldn't be any responses right now. I plugged my phone into its docking station speakers and selected my 'cleaning' playlist, turning up the volume whilst I cleaned my apartment, ready for Mamma's impending visit.

***

Friday! My favourite day of the week at work. Sure, it was identical to all of the other days, but if I made it through today I could be rewarded with two days off; even if one of those was with my mamma. She wasn't difficult to get along with, and we had a good mother/daughter relationship, but I preferred to slob around most weekends, or clear my head with a good hike. At least it would be a break from the usual routine.

Before I could even reach the weekend with Mamma, I still had to complete my usual chores; coffee pot, pastries, mail, but had resolved to call the Sandnes police station to obtain more information about Kari's arrest. It was by pure chance that Hansen announced that he'd be fetching his own lunch today and would be gone for around an hour. I was allowed to leave for lunch at 11:00, and headed straight for the coffee shop, choosing my usual food and hot chocolate. He left at around 11:30, insisting that I 'man' the office at all times until he returned. I wasn't disagreeable to this, as it gave me the perfect opportunity to make my phone calls. First, the local police station. The call connected swiftly, and I found myself speaking to Konstabel Pedersen, who had been first present at the 'crime scene'.

"The suspect was quite calm, and didn't resist arrest at all," he explained.

"What made you think that she had been the suspect then?" I asked.

"Well, the caller said she had murdered someone in the forest," he replied.

"But how do you know it was her? She could have been the victim..."

He laughed, "Murder victims don't usually present themselves so... so alive," he mocked.

I resisted the urge to lose my temper and probed him further. "The witness never described what the suspect, or indeed the victim, looked like, so I am suggesting that the murderer may still be at large."

"Ah, little girl, don't you worry your little head about these things. We are sure that we arrested the right person..." he trailed off as if to end the call.

"So, you found the victim, then?" I replied with an equally mocking tone.

"No, no, not yet," he mumbled, clearly unhappy at the checkmate.

"A murder weapon then? A confession? A written statement from the witness, maybe?" I pushed; I was on a roll! "Maybe you could send my little head a copy of the complete report, please?"

He muttered and moaned for far too long and finally agreed. Not that he could really refuse to give the defence lawyer vital information relevant to a murder case. I sat back in my chair and sighed contentedly, draining my hot chocolate and unsuccessfully throwing the cup into a distant bin. I stood up to retrieve it and place it into the bin and the phone rang. It was the first time in two weeks that the phone had rang so I rushed to answer it. It was Heidi, Mrs Hansen.

"I need to speak to Kenneth, Line," she spoke before I had the chance to.

"Hello Mrs Hansen, I'm afraid that Mr Hansen isn't in the office at the moment," I replied pleasantly.

"I know he is, because he left this morning, and he isn't at home," she replied snappily.

She wasn't the brightest tool in the toolbox. "No, Mrs Hansen, he popped out for lunch a short while ago. I can take a message and ask him to-"

"YOU WILL PUT ME THROUGH TO HIM RIGHT NOW," she screamed.

"Mrs Hansen, he's not...."

"YOUR PHONE HAS BEEN ENGAGED, SO I KNOW HE IS THERE."

Clearly she should have been a private investigator with those skills!

"Mrs. Hansen. It. Was. Me. On. The Phone. He. Isn't. Here. He. Popped. Out. For-"

She slammed the phone down. I stared at the phone, looking for answers that I wasn't going to get. Shaking my head, I mooched around the office, looking for things to do. I couldn't leave the office to replenish the coffee pot, so I returned to my desk again and refreshed the email inbox. Nothing. I sighed; this was going to be a long day.

I was wrong, as the phone rang again.

"Hello. Hansen and Associates," I greeted politely.

"My name is Konstabel Pedersen, was it you I was speaking to earlier?" the voice said.

"Yes, it was," I confirmed.

"Ah, ok, I was just checking. I need the address to send you the information about the Melshei Forest murder."

Despite his inability to be polite, I gave him the details and he hung up abruptly. People are so rude these days! I replaced the receiver and it immediately rang again. This time it was Heidi Hansen again, as equally fraught as the first time. I assured her that I'd let her precious husband know that she had rang - again! We had again gone through the process of her not believing he wasn't here, her assuming he was here when the phone was in use, and this time additionally questioning if Hansen was having an affair. I had explained that it was none of my business, which was apparently the wrong answer, as I was clearly covering up an illicit extra-marital fling. I kept my cool, it seemed to be part of my job description. Despite the neurotic wife, it was a pleasant change to be busy; I liked it. I clicked to refresh my emails and the phone rang again.

"Hello, H..."

"It's Agnes, Line," the caller cut in, to avoid the professional greeting.

"Hi, Agnes."

"I've got Heidi Hansen on the phone. She says she needs to speak to Mr Hansen," Aggie's voice was professional, which meant that Heidi could probably hear the conversation. I thanked her politely and again was faced with Hysterical Heidi.

"No, I do not want to speak to you," she greeted me, "you keep fobbing me off. Put me through to my husband's office."

"Hello Mrs Hansen, Mr Hansen isn't in his office."

"No, I am not talking to you. PUT ME THROUGH."

I transferred the call through to the empty office and let it ring. Hansen's answermachine kicked in after a few rings, and I could hear Heidi's voice say 'No,' and she hung up.

The routine of Heidi ringing me, Heidi ringing Aggie, and Heidi ringing Hansen's direct line completed the rest of my afternoon quite nicely. Each time she called it was with a little extra information; sometimes I was the mistress, sometimes it was Aggie, they had been robbed, had Kenneth been in a car accident? She had called hospitals and police who had suggested she ring his work, which she again did. Despite all this, Hansen never returned from his 'lunch'. I could only hope he was in a hospital…

I was glad it was Friday; I had the whole weekend ahead of me rather than dealing with Heidi again. I locked up all that I could, all that I had the keys to, turned off the coffee machine, grabbed my belongings and switched the lights off. I hummed absentmindedly down the stairs and as I approached the reception, I saw Aggie standing in front of her desk, with Heidi. I took this little opportunity to study the two women. Both had the similar traits of greying hair and the first signs of wrinkles. Heidi had dark circles under both eyes and looked more haggered and worn down than Aggie, despite the former being at least 10 years younger than Aggie.

I braced myself, smiled politely and continued to take the coffee pot into the kitchen, giving it a quick clean, then fetched my coat out of the cloakroom. I returned to the reception and attempted to leave the building, asking Aggie to lock the office for us.

"No," Heidi announced, "you are not leaving until I have been in the office to see Kenneth," she announced.

I couldn't be bothered to protest, so I suggested that I escort her up to the office and show her that he wasn't up there. She decided that it couldn't be her best option as I had offered too willingly, so she followed Aggie upstairs instead, insisting that I sit in the reception area until they returned. Satisfied that he wasn't in the office, Heidi returned to the reception but insisted that we both wait with her until her husband returned.

"Mrs Hansen," Aggie started, "Line has finished work for the week and has no obligation to stay, and I will be leaving shortly too. If you wish to wait for your husband, you will need to do so outside of the premises."

"How dare you!" Heidi screeched, "My husband is your boss, and you will do as I say!"

"Actually, Mrs Hansen, MY boss owns the building, and I maintain it for him, not your husband. And yes, although Line does work for Mr Hansen, this is only until 16:00. You are welcome to sit in reception until I have finished my duties for the day, but you will be leaving when I do, at the latest."

"But how do I know that she..." she pointed to me, "isn't off to meet my husband? I cannot allow this."

"I really couldn't care less, Mrs Hansen, and seeing as you can't seem to control your own husband, it is futile that you should attempt to control us too."

I did quite well at concealing my smirk, but felt an inner pride for Aggie. Sure enough, Heidi stormed off, trying to slam the slow-release door behind her. I congratulated Aggie and we laughed, but suddenly Heidi returned with a garden chair out of her car and set it up outside the building's doors. Aggie pulled one of her faces and decided to not do her usual cleaning, opting instead to leave when I did. Unfortunately for Heidi, the double doors opened inwards and as a result she wasn't obstructing us at all. Aggie opened the door and gestured for me to leave first. I walked around Heidi, as did Aggie once she had locked the doors. As we started to leave,

Hansen arrived, cursing and yelling at Heidi for making a scene, and we both made a break for it.

4 – Dark is the Night for All

We all laughed and joked about the spectacle that Heidi had made as I animatedly re-enacted my afternoon at the office to the girls.

"Where had he been, Line?" Astrid asked.

"I have absolutely no idea, and I couldn't care less," I laughed, sipping my wine.

We had chosen Italian tonight, at 'Luigi's', and were all gorging on pizza and pasta from their 'Friday buffet'.

"I have been doing old ladies' shampoo and sets all week," Astrid groaned.

"Well you did want to be a hair *stylist*, Astrid," Isabella laughed. "At least you get to talk to clients. I've been on coffee duty all week!"

"Well, my week hasn't been too grim actually, not wanting to gloat!" Helene announced, looking a little guilty with her 'success'. "How about you, Line?"

I nodded. "It has certainly been interesting," I smiled.

The girls all stared at me in anticipation.

"C'mon, Line, you can't leave us hanging like that!" Astrid groaned.

"Well," I started, "I'm not sure how much I should be telling you, due to confidentiality and all that jazz, so bear with me. Since I last saw you, I have bumped into my crush twice."

Before I could elaborate the girls were all interrupting, wanting all the juicy gossip.

"His name is Thorfinn, he was at the same school as me, and I loved him for about six years. Obviously, he didn't even know that I existed – or so I thought!" The girls gasped. "So, I went into a coffee shop on Sunday morning and he just appeared, and he knew me and my name!"

"So when are you going on a date then, Line?" Astrid butted in.

"No, we aren't going on any dates. He came to Oslo to get married! MARRIED! I was devastated, still am." The girls sighed in unified disappointment for me. "So, I text my sister and told her, and she rang me. When I was talking to her about Thor, he reappeared and that just made things worse." The girls gasped. "Then I saw him again in the week when I went to see Ingrid about a case I'm kinda working on."

"You have a case?" Belle asked.

"You saw him again?" Astrid enquired.

"The case is the bit I'm not sure if I can talk to you about or not, but yes, I saw Thor again, and no, we still aren't dating," I replied, pre-empting the next question from Astrid.

"Oh, that's a shame," Astrid sighed, "I'm sure we can sort that though."

"I am not getting involved with a married man, Astrid," I retorted; she sighed again.

"So, the case…," Helene prompted, "tell us what you can?"

"Hmmm," I thought briefly, "I'll keep it as general as I can then. So you all know how, erm, unprofessional Kenneth is?" They nodded, laughing amongst themselves. "Well, there is this new case, and I managed to get to tag along to the second visit in Halden last week. It's a murder case but the suspect won't talk – at all!"

"Isn't that how he should be, so that he doesn't incriminate himself?" Isabella watched a lot of crime dramas.

"She!" I replied, "*she* can talk to her lawyer, as he's bound to secrecy anyway. She looked so scared." I shook my head as I recounted the events.

"I thought Halden prison was for men only?" Helene probed.

"They merged with another prison during last year's lockdown, to save on staffing costs and reducing the risks of catching the virus," I explained, to the best of my ability.

"OK, so Kenneth has passed the case onto you then?" Belle frowned, trying to process the connection.

I laughed. "Hardly! He passed the case file to me to write up and arrange a court date for her. But... there's just something, I'm just not convinced she did anything..."

"So you are investigating it yourself?" Helene asked, incredulous.

I nodded. "It seems that way. Obviously Kenneth doesn't know anything about this. I spoke to Ingrid and she gave me a little advice, and I've done a little research for it too."

"WOW, Line! How lucky are you?!" Isabella replied, enviously.

"So far, I have managed to get a recording of the call made to emergency services, and am waiting for the report from the arresting officer. I just can't understand why she won't defend herself." I shook my head again.

"Well, I'm trained to be a journalist, which involves a lot of researching, so if you need me to help, I'd be delighted."

"Thanks, Tinkerbell. Thanks to all of you I suppose." I smiled at them appreciatively.

"Some girls get all the luck, eh?" Isabella grimaced.

"Not that lucky, if I can't even get my crush!" I laughed bitterly.

"Throw yourself into work, Line, at least you have a bit more than just the coffee and pastries!" Helene piped up.

We continued to eat and drink until the restaurant closed. I bid my friends goodbye and headed home.

5 – Between Your Mamma and Yourself

I was awoken abruptly by my doorbell ringing. I rolled over and looked at the time on my phone – shit! It was 11:00 and I was late meeting Mamma. I rolled out of bed and stumbled from my bedroom to the door, not quite making it in time to avoid the bell ringing again. I opened the door, and sure enough it was Mamma.

"Darling, why are you still in bed at this hour?"

"Morning, Mamma, I'm fine thanks, how are you?" I replied sarcastically.

"Morning? It's almost afternoon," she tapped her watch and breezed in, the smell of her perfume tickling my nose and triggering my hyperosmia. I sneezed repeatedly for several minutes until I had grabbed some toilet tissue from the bathroom and blown my nose. It was times like this that I regretted having my nose pierced, and was surprised that Mamma hadn't commented on it already. I switched the kettle on in the kitchen and pulled up a stool. Mamma sat on the other stool and was examining me thoroughly.

"So, how come you are in Oslo at the weekend, Mamma?' I asked, hoping to divert her attention away from her current thoughts, which I knew would be less than complimentary.

"Well, now that you girls are grown up, there's less need for me back up north."

"There's still Pappa," I replied, shocked by her lack of affection, which in itself was ridiculous as she had never been particularly affectionate at all.

"Yes, of course, but I thought I would go home tomorrow, as we are heading to Dubai on Monday. Besides, I wanted to see how my youngest child is settling into her own place." She looked around to study the cleanliness of the apartment. Thank goodness she didn't have white gloves, or she would probably have run them across the furniture and found very thick dust.

"Maybe you wouldn't sneeze so much if you cleaned your apartment more thoroughly, Line, dust particles are very bad for you." Ah, there we are! "And that nose thing doesn't help either." BINGO! That was some of her chosen topics ticked off the 'List of Disappointment'. "Have you even cleaned since you moved here, Line?"

In all fairness, I hadn't, and there was no point lying as she was the great lie detector of our family. I chose to simply ignore her last question, hoping it was rhetorical, and poured two fresh cups of coffee. Mum liked her coffee straight black, whereas mine was the opposite. I braced myself in anticipation of her next comment.

"You really shouldn't have all of that sugar, Line, it's not good for your teeth, or your weight."

"I do plenty of exercise," I risked lying, "and my dentist says my teeth are fine." Double lie!

I automatically rubbed my tongue along my front top teeth and felt the plaque; I hadn't been to the dentist since I started college, and she probably knew it. Change the subject, Line!

"So where are we going to for lunch today, Mamma?"

"I suppose you want nasty junk food," she remarked.

"Oh, no, I don't like junk food. It turns my stomach when I have to fetch it for my boss."

"Well, wherever we go, it'll probably be rather late for our lunch," she hinted, tapping her watch again.

I took the hint and took a slurp of my coffee before disappearing into the bathroom to get changed. I didn't have time for a shower but did manage a change of clothing, and my teeth and hair both got brushed. I slipped on my boots and gestured towards the door.

"Shall we?" I smiled, and Mamma rose gracefully from the chair and took her cup into the kitchen, quickly washing it, along with my cup and the cafetière. I was glad I had eaten out last night, otherwise there would have been more pots for her to silently judge whilst cleaning. Finally she had finished cleaning almost all of the kitchen and we were then on our way.

"I'm not sure who will still be open at this hour," she remarked, tapping her watch again.

'Maybe if you hadn't insisted on cleaning most of my home, it wouldn't be so late', I thought to myself. It wasn't even that late, and everywhere would be open. Mamma hailed a taxi. She had never seen the point of learning to drive as it was so much easier for her to commute and work on the way. She instructed the driver to take us to Apparatjik, one of the top places to eat in Oslo, apparently. As we arrived, we were greeted by, well, a greeter; he didn't seem to have any other function other than opening the door for us.

Entering the restaurant was a breathtaking experience. Compared to the coffee shops I had frequented, this was like a palace; not that I didn't love Marit's, of course. The ceiling was adorned with crystal chandeliers, but modern rather than the old-fashioned type. The exterior walls were mirrored, and the interior was glass. Mamma had never taken us anywhere to eat before, she preferred Pappa's home-cooked meals after a week of, well I guess it would be this; Apparatjik and the likes. The front desk host greeted Mamma by name and called for a less senior host to escort us to a table. All the chefs were on display at cooking stations around the restaurant, and even the tables were glass. Silver cutlery was tastefully adorned across the tables, along with crystal candelabra and white lily centrepieces. Even a royal wedding would be proud to have such a display! We took our seats and I stared at the glass menu that the host had passed to me. It may as well have been written in a foreign language, as I couldn't understand it at all. It was all impeccably written freehand and included dishes such as 'foams' of something, 'moody pools' of something else and even brain-meat!

"I see you are still unsophisticated, Line," Mamma laughed, gesturing to the gawping look on my face.

'Maybe if you had introduced us to this level of sophistication when we were younger, we wouldn't be so unsophisticated', I thought to myself.

"Shall I order for you, dear?" I nodded. "My usual, for two, Erik."

I had come to notice how rude those with money are, with Hansen's insolence and now Mamma's unfamiliarity despite being familiar with someone. I hadn't heard a simple please or thank you the entire day.

'Erik' waited patiently next to the table, a slight sparkle in his steely-blue eyes. 'I'm guessing he is waiting for a tip, like they do in movies', I thought.

"He's waiting for your menu, Line," she explained, before turning to Erik and explaining to him, how uncultured I was and laughing again.

I had a final glance at the menu and realised that there were no prices. 'I assume that it'd be a little too pricey to suggest to the girls', I laughed to myself.

"Thank you, Ms Larsen," he nodded and left promptly.

Erik soon returned with a bottle of champagne and two glasses. Of course, I should have guessed it would be champagne, although I don't think we had anything to celebrate, not that I was aware of at any rate. He showed Mamma the bottle and she nodded, then he poured a taster into one glass for her to try. She obliged and nodded. He then poured the light-coloured bubbly into both glasses and placed the remainder of the bottle into an ice bucket beside the table.

"Now sip this, dear, it's not like your cheap plonk!"

I took a small sip of the almost translucent beverage and the bubbles fizzed up my nose. I silently prayed that it wouldn't trigger a sneezing fit. It tasted disgusting, like what would be called dry, I suppose. I certainly was no wine connoisseur, and what I did drink was much sweeter than this. There was no 'I can taste sea air from Bordeaux along with woody cedar whatevers' for me. My mouth shrivelled up as I sipped it, and I soon returned the glass to the table as carefully as possible. I tried not to react too badly to the taste as it would just be further entertainment for my mother.

"So, Line, how is your new little job going?"

"Very well, thank you, Mamma."

She stared at me. "A little more information, Line?" she requested.

"Erm… well, I make coffee for my boss, and fetch pastries and lunch for him, and that's about it really." I had no intention of telling her all about Kari's case, I didn't trust her enough for that.

"Oh dear, is that all? Lillianne is doing so well advancing her career, and all that you got out of your *education* was a silly little job like that. Such a shame. You could have been a doctor, or a professor; anything would surely be better than that."

I didn't quite know how to respond. Should I agree with her?

Should I defend my 'silly little job'? Without elaborating on my new role, there was little that would suffice. Luckily we were interrupted by the fine frame of Erik, and the first course. Mamma had chosen a 'tasting platter'; a selection of small plates of food, exquisitely draped over several silver, glass, slate and wooden plates, dressed with edible flowers.

Before this moment, the only purple thing I had eaten was aubergine. I had no idea what this was or what it would taste like. Luckily, again, there was very little on each plate so I didn't have to endure much of any dish that was presented; I just did my best to smile and look like I was enjoying it. I declined more champagne and Mamma agreed it would be best, due to my low tolerance to alcohol. I had started to feel dizzy and over-warm after just a few sips.

Of all the plates, the very last one was my favourite, although I would never be able to describe it, apart from it being chocolatey but pink. Uncultured, you know! By this time, I was too full from all of those semi-empty plates to eat it all, which was a shame. I examined it, to see if I would be able to recreate it at home, for a fraction of the cost of course, but how on earth do you make pink chocolate?

I asked this question to Isabella later, when I called her to vent my anger a bit. Within half an hour she had appeared on my doorstep with decent, sweet wine, a bar of white chocolate and red food colouring. We spent the rest of the night drinking and attempting to make a pink chocolate dessert.

"So, did your Mamma tell you why she decided to visit you?" Belle asked me, as we tried to whizz up a little chocolate in my magic bullet machine to make a foam, which wasn't very magic, it seemed.

"Just a 'I'm in the area and thought I'd pop in' apparently. They're off to Dubai next week so she couldn't be bothered to rush home to her loving family. Thought she'd try and.... culture me, or something." The drink was going to my head.

Isabella was tapping into her phone to find a video showing us how to foam chocolate, but eventually we just decided to spoon the pink chocolate out of the bowl and ordered a pizza. Later that evening, Helene and Astrid arrived with another bottle of wine, and ice-cream.

"So, how uncultured are you then, Line?" Belle probed, to pique the interest of the others.

"Well, she kept saying 'unsophisticated', but...very," I slurred, with a spoon of ice-cream in my mouth. The girls laughed. "By the end of the 'very late lunch', Mamma decided to call us both a taxi as we were going in 'different directions' apparently." I tried to use the finger quotations gesture during my explanation, and this made them laugh even more.

"Oooh, 'different directions'," Belle mimicked me with her fingers, "that must have been VERY uncultured then!"

"How late was the 'very late lunch' then, Line?" Astrid asked, also mimicking my gestures.

"It was, like, 11:30 by the time she had finished washing up the coffee pots. Thank the gods she didn't see the dirty plates in the cupboard, otherwise it would have been dinner time!"

We all laughed.

***

"How drunk was I last night?" I asked Bella the next morning - well, afternoon - after dragging my hungover ass out of bed.

"Not bad at all," she replied, smiling. "How much do you

remember?"

"Erm... we had pizza, ice cream, wine and pink chocolate?"

"So you don't remember the shots and the slideshow of pictures of Thor?"

"No..."

"It's all ok," she reassured, "you didn't embarrass yourself. We all need to vent sometimes, and last night was your turn. I guess you don't remember the karaoke then?"

"Please tell me that I didn't attempt to sing?"

"The neighbours only banged on the ceiling once," Belle laughed, passing me a cup of coffee.

We lounged around the apartment for the rest of the day, and I let Belle listen to the mp3 recording. I'd already written down most of the questions that she raised, and we were still at a loss.

"I'll see what comes through from the arresting officer and see if I can make any sense of it."

"Please keep me up to date with this, Line, I love stuff like this."

It was true, Belle always managed to work out who the suspect was in any crime movie or tv series, whereas I was always rubbish at it.

6 – The Wake

"Bright and early again, Line?" Aggie greeted me.

"Yes! Lots of work to do this week," I replied.

"Work?" she pulled a face. "Does he need more coffee than usual then?" she cackled.

"I'm doing my own little investigation," I explained, putting a finger to my lips.

"Ahh," she replied, tapping her nose, "Mum's the word!"

"Hmmmm…" I replied, "Talking of 'witch', my mamma visited me on Saturday. She took me to Apparatjik for lunch, but unfortunately I'm way too unsophisticated for her!"

"Apparatjik?! WOW, your mum must be very rich then?"

"High-powered businesswoman, with a high-powered credit card!"

"Lovely," Aggie responded, nodding her head to indicate that Hansen was here.

I'd been so distracted with talk of Thor and Kari that I'd completely forgotten the Hansens' saga.

"Larsen," Hansen nodded as he approached the reception, and handed a cheque to Aggie. I nodded back and went about my business.

I waited for most of the day for gossip about Friday's incident but had no joy. Not even any mail from the police station yet either. I was on a bit of a downer by the end of the day, so decided that I needed a 'pick me up', a hot chocolate from Marit's. Much to my disapproval, it started raining and I had left my raincoat at home, opting for my fluffy red coat instead; BIG MISTAKE! Luckily, Marit found a spare stool and placed it by the counter, but out of the way of other customers. I sat there, hugging my hot chocolate and observed the other customers as they entered. Most stomped their feet dry on the mat by the door, some stood with the door open and shook their umbrellas outside. Marit had a handy coat and umbrella holder by the door, which was appreciated by her patrons, but lack of table space meant that a lot of customers had takeaway orders instead. I thought how great her little business was, she must earn quite a bit, seeing how busy it always seemed to be. I realised that I had used my mother's phrase 'little business' like 'little job'; I shuddered and shook myself to clear the image of me as a fifty-year-old woman with no heart.

As the rush seemed to die down a bit, Marit came over to talk to me for a short while, with a fresh hot chocolate – her treat. We were chatting about Hansen when the devil himself walked in. I hid around the corner of the counter, as I didn't want him to see me. As he approached the counter, he started to be quite flirty with Marit. My stomach turned but she just smiled politely and gave him his drink and cake. I saw him as he watched her walk away from him, and seemed to congratulate himself on some victory that was only apparent to him. He turned around when a lady called him over; despite the kiss he gave her as they met, this most certainly was NOT Heidi!

***

"My husband works hard to keep a roof over your head, as well as ours..." Heidi ranted over the phone the next afternoon. "He doesn't get home until late at night, you know, so you should be grateful that you are allowed to leave so early."

Clearly that – whoever the woman at Marit's was yesterday – was not classed as 'work', but who was I to contradict? I was happy to let them get on with it if it meant I could have an easier life. It's only a 'little job' anyway!

Apparently, the Hansen house was robbed on Friday, and Mrs H had only rang so many times because she needed to call Hansen to check who to call. If I had known this apparent situation, I would have told her to call the police, then the insurance people, but seeing how rude she was to me, no, I probably wouldn't have told her actually! I didn't know whether to pity her or slap her to knock some sense into her. Sure, she was right about him possibly cheating on her, but there were better ways to check without ranting at, and accusing, his colleagues/staff. Hansen's office door remained closed as he yelled at and patronised his wife, and I wondered if she was really that stupid, or had she been burned before?

I clicked 'refresh' on my emails, as I seemingly did hundreds of times a day. I looked up at the clock; 15:58. Lovely, time to close the computer down… Suddenly, Hansen appeared at my desk.

"Any emails, Larsen?"

"No, I just checked before I switched the comput.."

"Well, switch it back on and check again." I sat in silence, hoping for a please which was nowhere in sight. "Well?" he asked impatiently.

"It's just loading up again," I lied.

I waited for the emails to open again and turned the screen around so that he could see that there were no emails.

"Dammit! When is that court date going to come through!" he chastised nobody in particular. "You definitely sent through the Nordmann case, Larsen?"

"Yes, Mr Hansen," I lied.

He sighed again and paced round the office.

"I can check with them tomorrow if you like?" I offered.

"Yes," he said through gritted teeth, "do that!"

I smiled and switched the computer off again.

Feeling a little stressed about the situation, I felt the need for a hot chocolate and headed to Marit's. The place was packed to the rafters and I couldn't see a spare space to sit, so figured I would have to take it home with me. I stood in the queue and waited patiently for my turn, and as I approached the counter a man dodged in front of me, jumping the queue. With the mood I was in I had no intention of letting someone get away with that.

"Hey, I've been queuing ages for this, get to the back, loser," I ranted.

"Miss 'Unsophisticated'!" he growled back, and turned around to face me.

His face seemed familiar, but I couldn't place him.

"I'll pay for this lady's order, Marit," he smiled, handing her a credit card. "This way, Miss," he gestured towards the table he had leapt away from to queue-jump and that's when I recognised him.

"You are the guy who served us at Apparatjik at the weekend?" I questioned rather than stated; faces weren't my speciality.

"Erik, Miss," he smiled again, pulling the chair out for me to sit.

"Enough with the formalities please, Erik. The name is Line."

"Sure thing, Miss Line," he smiled.

I grimaced. "So, how often does my mother frequent your restaurant, Erik?" I eventually asked, after picking all of the marshmallows off the hot chocolate one by one and eating them.

"She *frequents* quite often, takes a lot of clients there to celebrate deals, it seems."

I could feel him watching me, and became aware that I may have had cream on my nose. I was correct, I realised as I rubbed a little tissue over it until it was clear. Erik's eyes seemed to sparkle as he smiled at me.

"Aren't you meant to discreetly inform people of things like that?" I asked, blushing.

"I'm not working now, Miss Line."

The conversation continued to flow until Marit announced that she was closing the coffee shop, and we vacated willingly. On the short, and intentionally slow walk back to my apartment we chatted further.

"This is my place," I announced as we stopped outside my apartment block.

There was a short pause and then Erik walked towards me, holding my gaze. He outstretched his arm and I felt my mouth going dry.

"Line," he whispered.

"Yes," I whispered back.

"Here's my phone, type your number in it if you want me to call you sometime."

The pause for a response was only a few seconds, but seemed like forever. I took the phone, typed in my number and handed it back. As I did so, he grabbed my hand gently, pulled me towards him and kissed me gently.

"Good night, Miss Unsophisticated."

***

As soon as I entered my apartment, I threw off my boots and spun around a few times, smiling broadly. My phone beeped.

'See you soon, Miss U?'

It was a text from Erik. Miss U…? He misses me already?! My heart started beating faster, I could feel the pulse in my ear. I started texting back, 'Miss U 2' when I realised he meant Miss Unsophisticated. That could have been a big no-no if I hadn't cottoned on quickly enough. I deleted my unsent reply and sat down to think about it at length. I didn't want to seem too keen, but also wasn't keen on leaving it for too long. My bestie would know! I clicked speed dial number 1 and waited for her to answer.

"What am I going to do, Tinkerbell?" I asked, and explained all that had happened that evening.

She was very happy for me, my increasing obsession with a married man wasn't a good move for me. We laughed together at my potential faux pas following Erik's text, and decided that I should text him once we finished our call.

"How is the case going, Line?" Belle probed.

I explained the situation with the files. "I've told Hansen that I've sent the report off, but I haven't. Maybe I just need to forget all about this and let it be resolved as it should be, in court."

"Surely there is some way that you can hold off for a little longer?"

"Unless some miracle shows itself, no," I replied despondently.

"Sleep on it, Line, you never know!"

I found myself pacing round my apartment like Hansen did at work; I'd need to stop that habit!

***

I had a restless night and was up quite early the next morning. By the time I had showered, dressed and had several coffees, I had decided to leave it for the professionals to do their job. If Kari was innocent, she should speak up and tell them. It wasn't up to me, a mere secretary in a shoddy law firm, to sort out. There were many officials in the position to help more than I could. As I was leaving the apartment, I received a text from Isabella.

'WHAT DID YOU DECIDE? X'

She knew exactly what I was like! We had been best friends since before school, had gone to the same after-school activities together, then to Oslo for college.

'I'VE DECIDED TO LEAVE IT TO THE PROFS. WILL RING YOU LATER FROM WORK, IF THAT'S OK? X'

I grabbed my raincoat, just in case, and left for work. Sure enough, the rain poured all the way to the office. People were running around randomly, like they had never been out in the rain before. Darting for shelter under nearby shop signs and in doorways. These same people were disrupting the daily commute for others with their selfishness, it made my blood boil.

"Are you ok, Line?" Aggie enquired when I arrived.

"Yes thanks, Agnes. I'm just getting agitated about things I can't control again!" She pulled a face and it made me laugh. "Thank you, Aggie. In a world full of idiots, it's great to be with someone who is normal."

"Don't you dare judge me as being 'normal'!" she smiled, and carried on wiping windows and watering her plants, singing to herself.

I hung my wet raincoat up and grabbed the coffee pot. Aggie was still singing as I ventured upstairs to see what shit storm awaited me today.

Hansen was way ahead of me, already puffing his way around his little office space, on his mobile phone. I sorted the coffee pot out and locked my bag in my drawer. I switched the computer on and found zero new messages, as expected. I just hoped that my plan would work out ok. I pulled out the folder from my desk drawer, and opened it to the court document, and dialled Isabella's number instead of the court.

"Hey, Line, what's the plan?" Belle greeted me.

"Good morning, my name is Line Larsen and I work for Mr Hansen, from Hansen and Associates," I replied.

"Ok, I'll run with this," Belle laughed.

"Mr Hansen has asked me to check the status of one of his client's court dates, if you could help me, please?"

"You are naughty, Line," Belle replied.

"Oh, I see. You've had a problem with your fax machine?"

"Seriously, who uses fax machines these days, haha, it's the 21st century for crying out loud."

"Oh, ok, thank you, I will mail the form to you instead. Thank you again."

"Smart lady, buys you a few extra days, eh?"

"Yes, thank you again for all your help."

"You're welcome, sweetie."

I tried to restrain my victory dance, as I could feel Hansen watching me.

"Make sure you take a photocopy of that document, rather than sending off the original."

'Way ahead of you there, Hansen', I thought to myself. I dutifully photocopied the document and popped it into an envelope. I skipped down the stairs happily and sat in the reception area, waiting for Aggie to finish a phone call.

"Just one letter for you today, Line," Aggie said, startling me.

I smiled. "And just one for you, Agnes." I handed her the letter. "Now, if this is going to get you into any trouble, then ignore my request, but is there any chance you could keep this letter for a day or two, to delay it please?"

"Is it another rubber cheque from Mr H?" she laughed.

Every month, Hansen paid for the rental of the office by cheque, and always a few days after the due date. Coincidentally, each month the cheque bounces and it has to be presented at the bank again. It must cost him a fortune in bank charges, but I wasn't even going to attempt to delve into his finances. If it affected Aggie's wages then I would try and rectify it, but she had assured me on numerous occasions that it didn't.

"No, it is more of a favour for me. It's this client I've been wanting to help. I feel that she may not be guilty but Hansen is more than happy to collect the plea deal and his small fee, rather than investigate on the off-chance that he can get more money."

"So you are trying to help him to earn more money?" she pulled a quizzical face.

I laughed. "Noooo! Just can't stand the injustice of it all, it's frustrating!"

"Ok, I shall mail it Friday, so that it has a couple of days in the postal system before they receive it?"

"That sounds great. Can you remind me before you send it, please?"

"Sure will, Captain," she saluted me as I skipped back upstairs.

Back at my desk, I studied the envelope and realised it was addressed to me. I slid it under my 'in tray' so that I could open it when Hansen was busy. As it goes with these situations, it seems like Hansen has a sixth sense and always hovers close by when there's something 'afoot', as he calls it. Luckily, he received a call and disappeared into his office, shutting the door on his way. I slid the envelope from under the tray containing zero work to be done, and carefully opened it. It was from the Sandnes police officer. My heart started beating rapidly and my mouth went a little dry. I glanced above my desk and saw that Hansen was making for his door. I quickly shoved everything back in its envelope and sat on it. Trying to look calm and composed, I smiled weakly.

"I have to go out for the rest of the day, Larsen, so if you need anything for lunch you had better fetch it now, as I need you to stay here and keep an eye on things."

I looked up at the clock. It was 09:47. "Sure, I will go in just a sec then. I assume you don't want any pastries whilst I am there?"

He pondered this thought. "Just a couple of the chocolate ones, I suppose." He placed some money on my desk. "Don't forget my receipt."

Had I ever forgotten his receipt since the first time?! "Ok, will do."

I leaned over and unlocked my desk drawer to retrieve my bag, and luckily he had wandered back into his office for another cigarette. I popped the envelope into the drawer and locked it.

Picking up his money, I whisked out of the office before he could change his mind. It was still raining when I reached the reception, so I went to the cloakroom to grab my coat. It was quite damp on the inside and a little uncomfortable.

"Take my umbrella, if you like?" Aggie appeared from nowhere.

"Do you have a sixth sense too, Aggie?"

"Too? Who else has my 'woman's intuition'?"

I laughed. "Hansen!"

"HAHA He wouldn't know intuition if it bit him on the…"

"Ah good, Larsen, I haven't missed you. Could you grab me a bacon roll too?" He shoved a few more notes into my hand.

"That was a bit close, Aggie!" I mock-chided her.

"Yes, but my 'woman's intuition' stopped me in time."

"That it did, Agnes," I smiled and headed to Marit's.

It was remarkably quiet in the coffee shop this morning, probably because it was too early for lunch. I found my obsessing about an 'early lunch' on a par with Mamma's 'late lunch', thank the gods I wasn't tapping my watch.

"Good morning, Line. How was your evening after I closed up last night?" Marit beamed at me.

"Oh! I completely forgot to reply to his text!" I cried, a little too loud.

"Well take a seat and REPLY, Line! Pastries?"

"He only wants a couple of chocolate ones today please, and a bacon roll."

"Ok, no problem." She turned away and started preparing the roll, and I browsed the selection that were ready to purchase, scrunching my nose up at the limited options.

"What's with the face, Line?" a voice appeared from behind me.

"Thor!"

"Line!" he mocked. "Nothing you fancy?"

Now there was a double-edged sword.... "Hmmm... I don't usually come here so early for my lunch, and I'm not sure what's going to hit the mark."

"How about soup?" Marit suggested. "Carrot and coriander, your favourite." She wafted the spoon that she had been stirring it with under my nose.

"Mmmmmm that sounds delicious, but we don't have a microwave to heat it up."

"Erm... ok then," Marit pondered for a few minutes. "I can make up your favourite salmon and cream cheese when the queue has died down a bit."

I looked around me, and indeed, a queue had formed in the time it had taken me to not make my mind up at all. I became a little flustered.

"Blimey, where did all of those people come from? They weren't here a few minutes ago!"

"The train," Marit explained.

"Ah, well, I won't keep you any longer, just these bits for the boss, please."

"OK, Line. Don't forget the text message," she prompted me, nodding at the phone in my hand.

We exchanged money and goods and I said goodbye to both of them, before rushing out. Back at the office, I discovered that Marit had slipped an extra package in with my goods, an extra pastry. It was a good job I noticed instead of just handing it all to Hansen. That would have to do for lunch. Luckily, I was planning to have a busy day once he left the office, so that would take my mind off the food. He allowed me just enough time to freshen up the coffee pot, mainly because he wanted his travel mug filling up though. I managed to fill a second coffee pot with water to top it up later and keep me going for the afternoon. Once Hansen had disappeared in a cloud of cigarette smoke, I grabbed myself a coffee and stood by the window for a few minutes, to make sure that he had definitely left. 'Let's hope I don't end up with psycho-Heidi this afternoon', I thought to myself, as I spotted his car exiting from the car park. 'Bye bye, Kenneth!'.

Once I had finished my coffee, I refilled my cup and returned to my desk, retrieving the envelope out of my drawer. I rummaged through my bag until I found my phone, and selected a playlist to listen to. 'As long as it doesn't interfere with my work, it won't be a problem', I assured myself. Aggie would be on automatic standby to let me know if Hansen came back early, allowing me time to restore to normality. I composed a reply to Erik's text and breathed a sigh of relief.

I took another deep breath before I pulled the paperwork out of the envelope. The first entry was for the first response made by the officers, following the report to the emergency services about the incident.

<u>FIRST RESPONSE REPORT</u>

1 OCTOBER

13:08 - CALL MADE BY UNKNOWN FEMALE TO EMERGENCY SERVICES. WITNESS STATES THAT POSSIBLE MURDER COMMITTED IN 'THE FOREST', BUT LOCATION NOT CONFIRMED.

13:12 - CALL TRACED TO PAYPHONE NEARBY TO MELSHEI FOREST AND SANDNES FIRST RESPONDERS DISPATCHED.

14:28 - FIRST RESPONDERS ARRIVE AT SCENE. ONE YOUNG FEMALE SEATED ON BENCH NEAR BUS STOP. OFFICERS APPROACHED WITH CAUTION AND DISCOVERED HER TO BE MID 20s WITH A GREAT DEAL OF BLOOD ABOUT HER PERSON.

14.34 - SUSPECT CAUTIONED AND TAKEN TO SANDNES POLICE STATION FOR QUESTIONING.

DESK SERGEANT

1 OCTOBER

15:02 - SUSPECT [NO NAME] - FEMALE, MID 20s - AND KONSTABEL PETERSEN ARRIVE AT STATION. SUSPECT CONSENTS TO A FULL SEARCH, TO BE CARRIED OUT BY FEMALE OFFICER.

15:22 - FEMALE KONSTABEL SEARCHES SUSPECT - NO WEAPON OR IDENTIFICATION ON SUSPECT. DNA ORAL SWABS TAKEN. BLOOD SAMPLES TAKEN FROM SUSPECT'S CLOTHING AND UNDER FINGERNAILS. GROUND DIRT ALSO FOUND UNDER NAILS AND SENT OFF TO LAB FOR TESTING.

15:53 - SUSPECT REFUSES TO TALK, PLACED IN HOLDING CELL FOR FURTHER QUESTIONING.

----

2 OCTOBER

14:55 - ON CALL COURT-APPOINTED DEFENCE ATTORNEY - KENNETH HANSEN OF HANSEN AND ASSOCIATES ARRIVES. ACCESS GRANTED IN INTERVIEW ROOM 2.

15:20 - OVERKONSTABEL NILSEN PERFORMS FORMAL INTERVIEW WITH SUSPECT IN INTERVIEW ROOM 2, WITH COURT-APPOINTED DEFENCE ATTORNEY, MR KENNETH HANSEN OF HANSEN AND ASSOCIATES, IN ATTENDANCE. MR HANSEN DID NOT NEED TO ADVISE SUSPECT TO REMAIN SILENT.

I was jolted back to reality by a phone call.

"Good…" I looked up at the clock to check the time. It was 11:30., "aft…"

"Line, It's Aggie."

"Is he back already?"

"No, but there is a very handsome young man in reception, asking to see you."

I frowned. "I'm not allowed out of the office whilst Hansen is away," I explained.

"I can intercept the calls for a few minutes, I'm sure," she assured me.

"Ok, I'll be right down."

I popped my bag back into my desk drawer, filed all the paperwork back into the envelope and locked all items securely away. Grabbing the coffee pot, I gingerly walked downstairs, wondering who my handsome visitor was, hoping it was Erik. Knowing Aggie, it was probably a homeless man or something, not that we saw many of those in Oslo.

"Hi again, Line," my mystery man said.

"Thor!" I smiled and felt myself blush.

"I brought you a little something," he explained, and pulled a pot of soup out of the brown paper bag he was carrying. "Carrot and coriander, right?"

My heart melted and I was speechless.

"I'll get you a couple of spoons," Aggie announced.

When she returned we were still just looking at each other. "I'd suggest that you eat it down here, but you know what the boss is like." I tore my eyes away from this gorgeous specimen of a man to respond with a grunt. "Maybe Sir, erm Thor, would accompany you upstairs, Line?"

"Sure, I have a bit of spare time before my next lecture," Thor answered for me, smiling dreamily.

We took the elevator up to the office, not wanting to spill the soup. Thor sat down in the chair next to my desk and poured some of the soup into two mugs that Aggie had shoved into his hands, passing one to me. I could hardly taste the flavour, as I was too lost in Thor's beautiful blue eyes.

"So, how is your case going?"

"My case?"

"Yes, last week you were telling Ingrid about a case you were looking into."

"Oh, THAT case! Ha ha. It's …. developing. I don't want to say too much, client confidentiality and all that!" I tapped my nose and winked.

"Sure, I understand."

We ate our soup in silence, only hindered by the phone.

"Good…."

"Mr Hansen is back, Line," Aggie's voice interrupted my greeting.

"Crap! Thanks, Aggie."

"What's wrong?" Thor enquired, concerned by my level of flapping.

"The boss will be here any second."

"Relax, Line, I have a contingency plan. Just follow my lead."

Mr Hansen burst through the door, and Thor stood up to greet him.

"Who are you?" Hansen questioned, looking back and forth between Thor and myself.

"Mr Hansen," Thor began, oustretching his arm for a formal handshake, "my name is Thorfinn Valle. I'm studying law at the local college…" he continued to talk despite Hansen walking off. "I'm here with a copy of my credentials, and am looking for some work…"

Hansen cut him off. "No, unfortunately I'm not in a position to hire anyone right now. Give your 'credentials' to Larsen and I'll contact you if anything changes."

"Mr Hansen," Thor continued. "This is FREE work experience. I'd be your general dogsbody for two weeks. It's just so I can gain some on-the-job experience, rather than just in a lecture hall."

Hansen stopped dead in his tracks. "Oh, ok," you could almost see the dollar signs in his eyes, like in the cartoons. "Well, still give your details to Larsen and I'll give you a call to talk about it further tomorrow, if that suits?"

"Yes, Mr Hansen, I am in a lecture from…."

"Tell Larsen everything we need to know and we'll sort. I only came in to grab something. Maybe we can chat on the way back down though?"

"Sure thing. Here's my *credentials,* Miss Larsen, thank you both for your time." He handed me an A4 sheet of paper and smiled as he followed Hansen.

"I'll be out for the rest of the day, Larsen," Hansen shouted back as the door sprang shut.

I walked to the window and watched them both leave. Returning to my seat, I refreshed the coffee machine and then just sat for a while, spinning my chair and grinning like a Cheshire cat.

***

I looked at the clock and it was now 14:02. Back to work!

I re-scanned the document to try and find the place where I had been disturbed. 'What a lovely disturbance', I thought.

"Ah," I said out loud, but to myself. I was half-way through 2nd October by the looks of it.

16:10 - SUSPECT REFUSES TO COMMENT. SENT BACK TO HOLDING CELL UNTIL TRANSFER TO HALDEN. MR HANSEN CONFIRMS THAT THE SUSPECT DID NOT ATTEMPT TO TALK WITH HIM PRIOR TO FORMAL INTERVIEW.

----

3 OCTOBER

16:30 - SUSPECT TRANSFERRED TO HALDEN.

Next was the report of the officers who were searching Melshei Forest for a victim, or evidence of a victim.

2 OCTOBER

OVERKONSTABEL PETERSEN ALONG WITH KONSTABELS DAHL, GAMST, DAMMEN, KLEVE, SKAGEN AND LUND BEGIN COMBING THE AREA OF MELSHEI FOREST TO LOOK FOR CLUES AND VICTIM OF SUSPECTED MURDER ON 1 OCTOBER. NO EVIDENCE DISCOVERED.

3 OCTOBER

OVERKONSTABEL PETERSEN ALONG WITH KONSTABELS DAHL, KALBERG, DAMMEN, KLEVE, SKAGEN AND LUND CONTINUE COMBING THE AREA OF MELSHEI FOREST TO LOOK FOR CLUES AND VICTIM OF SUSPECTED MURDER ON 1 OCTOBER. ONE [1] GREY SOCK FOUND IN GRID B4 OF SEARCH MAP.

4 OCTOBER

OVERKONSTABEL PETERSEN ALONG WITH KONSTABELS DAHL, GAMST, DAMMEN, KLEVE, SKAGEN AND LUND CONTINUE COMBING THE AREA OF MELSHEI FOREST TO LOOK FOR CLUES AND VICTIM OF SUSPECTED MURDER ON 1 OCTOBER.

ROPE FOUND AT TREE ROOT LEVEL IN GRID D11 OF SEARCH MAP.

5 OCTOBER

OVERKONSTABEL PETERSEN NOT AVAILABLE. SEARCH LED BY OVERKONSTABEL NILSEN, ALONG WITH KONSTABELS DAHL, GAMST, DAMMEN, KLEVE, SKAGEN AND LUND CONTINUE COMBING THE AREA OF MELSHEI FOREST TO LOOK FOR CLUES AND VICTIM OF SUSPECTED MURDER ON 1 OCTOBER.

6 OCTOBER

SEARCH LED BY OVERKONSTABELS PETERSEN AND NILSEN CONCLUDE THAT NO PHYSICAL EVIDENCE FOUND RE: MELSHEI FOREST MURDER ON 1 OCTOBER.

7 OCTOBER

LAB REPORT CONFIRM THAT 1 [ONE] GREY SOCK RECOVERED NOT RELEVANT TO MELSHEI MURDER ON 1 OCTOBER

8 OCTOBER

FINDINGS CONCLUDE THAT ROPE EVIDENCE PRE-DATES MURDER ENQUIRY BY APPROXIMATELY 17 MONTHS.

I photocopied all of the documents that I had received and put the original paperwork neatly back into the envelope again. I needed somewhere to store all of this new evidence, so I could look at it without any suspicion. I would use the copied documents to make notes as I thought of them.

The phone rang.

"Good af…"

It's me, Line," Aggie's husky voice cackled as she laughed. "You know it's 16:10? Why are you still here?"

"I had no idea it was so late! I'll be there in 5!"

Just as I was leaving, I returned to my desk drawer and took the original documents out of their envelope. I grabbed a new envelope from the stationery cupboard and used that to store them instead, as it would cause much less suspicion than having something with my name at the office address on, if Hansen happened to go rifling through my drawers.

***

That evening, my head was crammed with information; Erik hadn't replied to my text yet, maybe I had left it too late - unintentionally played it too cool. Thor had come forward and made a move, but he was married. Kari, I had made fantastic progress with her case, the information had flooded through already.

I was so tired. I had such an exhausting couple of days that I crawled straight into bed and was asleep in minutes.

***

I needed a long shower to shake off the fatigue the next morning, and have to admit that I checked my phone for a reply to my text to Erik far too many times. I peered through my bedroom window, adorned with only a towel, to judge the weather. The office was heated but with Hansen leaving the windows open most of the day, I decided to layer up. A high-neck top, to avoid any cleavage issues, was standard since I had worked there, and I chose a dove grey v-neck tank top over the white shirt that I had selected. Trousers were again a must-have in the office, for the same reasons as the high-neck top, and as the shirt covered most of my assets I decided to be daring with slightly tighter-fitting trousers, in a darker grey than the tank top. I applied a more liberal layer of makeup than usual, but nothing to give my employer the 'wrong impression'. I felt good today, mainly due to my male admirers.

Attracting the boys at school was near-on impossible, I was never the popular child at any point in my education, and my infatuation with Thor made me appear more aloof and unapproachable. It was my sister, Lillianne, who had all the attention. I landed the odd 'pity-date' for those whose friends wished to date Lilli; rather like double dating without being out together at the same time. I think this was something that Lilli had insisted upon, to allow me the opportunity to have some male attention. The 'boys' I had been handed were clearly in the same boat as me, paired up with the loser mate of Lilli's admirer. She wore makeup from an early age, a lot sooner than I did at fifteen. Her skirt was hiked up to a little lower than her bottom and her shirt was unbuttoned equally as provocatively.

My clothes were always the opposite, high-necked and low skirts, below my knees. My medium brown hair was always tied back in a simple ponytail, her blonde hair was always loose and carefree, rather like Lilli! She oozed all the confidence of Mamma, whereas I was left with Pappa's genes and lack of self-confidence. I admired him and his life ethics; happy to stay at home and look after us rather than pursue a career of his own. Before we came along, he was quite prominent in the community, working as a local schoolteacher. He could have continued his career once we arrived, but felt that we needed a permanent parent at home whilst Mamma worked away so much. Pappa always encouraged us to follow a path that would make us happy, whereas Mother attempted to steer us in a direction that suited her. As a top bod in a pharmaceutical company, no-one could ever match Mamma's income.

She had attempted to nudge both of us into a medical career from an early age, buying Lilli children's doctor dress-up kits ahead of her age range, and passing them onto me when the latest suitably educational toy appeared on the market. Lilli had done her best at medical college. When she ungracefully 'dropped out' after one term, due to her being unable to tolerate blood, the whole incident was swept under the carpet and she was steered towards translation work, using her natural ability of picking up languages much easier than I ever could.

I too chose not to pursue medicine and seemed to be following in my father's footsteps, which he supported and assisted as much as possible, much to Mamma's disapproval. It was only when I started to show an interest in law that she stepped in and tried to push me into the local university of law, with a view to me becoming a professor, of course. Pappa always encouraged us to choose a path that made us happy, rather than one that made Mamma happy. 'It's your life', he'd tell us. The more Mamma drove us to succeed, the more Lilli tried to please her, and I pulled back with equal determination. Once school was over, the family dynamics had shifted; I became the rebellious one with piercings and tattoos whilst Lilli became the 'yes man'. I never regretted any of my decisions from that point on.

I finished dressing, slurped the last of my coffee and wrapped myself up ready for the bitter elements outside. Slipping my phone into my coat pocket, I popped my earphones in and grabbed my bag. Today's playlist had been labelled as 'motivational' and I felt on top of the world by the time I reached work. Despite my phone being programmed to interrupt me if I had received a text, I found myself checking it anyway, hoping for a message from Erik. I tried to not let his lack of contact affect my mood, beaming at Aggie as I entered the reception area. She was still wearing her scarf and gloves, nursing a hot drink to keep warm. We had a brief conversation about the weather, and she poured me a coffee as I unloaded my top layers into the cloakroom. I sat with her for a few minutes until Hansen arrived. I drained my cup, grabbed the fresh coffee pot and raced him to the office, purely to reinstate my victorious mood.

Mail, pastries and emails sorted, I was now facing a lull in my workload. I refilled my coffee mug, not that I needed more caffeine running through my system, and impatiently paced the office. This pattern set the scene for the whole morning. Hansen had his office door open the whole time and he sat with his feet up on the desk, texting on his mobile phone, snorting to himself every now and then. The lunch run was a welcome relief from the mundane, and I didn't care how cold it was outside. I intentionally fetched Hansen's food first, not caring if it was cold when I got back to the office. I wasn't prepared to sacrifice my hot chocolate temperature for that slob. I queued for what seemed like an eternity. As I got nearer to the counter, there was a couple debating what their child could and couldn't have. I rolled my eyes. The old lady in front of me stepped forward, her confusion of not knowing what burger to have draining my patience further. I was silently calculating who would finish first when the till that has served the young couple became available. I stepped forward, as the man of the young couple turned around. It was Erik.

Our eyes were locked for a second and he smiled at me, before the woman called him away to help with a highchair for the child. He turned away briefly and I made a break for it, almost knocking over the further-confused pensioner. Apologising profusely, I ensured that she was steady on her feet and her food was balanced. Not satisfied, I carried the tray and helped her find a seat. Not wanting to look back at Erik, I disappeared out of the restaurant swiftly. Although I was sure that Erik wouldn't leave his family, I didn't want to hang around to find out and picked up the pace, automatically heading for Marit's. The queue wasn't particularly short here either, but at least it wouldn't upset me further. I had no plan of how to resolve this issue and was still pondering it when I got a tap on my shoulder. With a great intake of breath, I slowly turned round to face whoever it was. It was a relief to find Astrid beaming at me.

"Is this one of your regular places, Line?" she asked me.

I nodded, trying to keep my composure. I couldn't fool Astrid though, and she pulled me out of the queue, asking the lady behind me to save my place for a minute.

"What's wrong?" she asked with genuine concern.

"It's a long story," I replied.

"Well, I have an hour for my lunch break."

"I don't," I explained. "I still have to get H… Kenneth his burger."

"Ok?"

"There's someone in there that I don't want to be near."

Astrid frowned. "Ok, then I shall get it for you. You stay in the queue and order our food and I will bring Kenneth's food back and wait here for you whilst you drop it off. How does that sound?"

I nodded, trying to blink back the tears. She told me what she wanted, and I told her Hansen's order.

"H… He needs a receipt, please."

"Sure, I will make sure I get one. See you shortly."

She physically returned me to the queue thanking the lady behind me, and speedily left the coffee shop. I was grateful for the slow-paced queue in Marit's, as it gave Astrid more time to clear the 'fast food' queue. I fought back the tears again when Marit asked me what was wrong. I assured her it was nothing serious and gave her our order. She gave me our drinks and I stood hopelessly at the counter looking for somewhere to sit. I was still there when Astrid returned, proffering Hansen's food bag. We swapped places and I rushed to the office to drop it off. I gave him his receipt and muttered something about the queues being bad and whizzed back out of the door before he could complain. Back at Marit's, Astrid had acquired a table, and the food arrived when I did.

"Ok, spill," Astrid broke the silence.

I explained everything as we ate our open sandwiches; the restaurant, the kiss, the texts and finally the new family developments, and she listened without judgement. I had managed to control my crying to a gentle, silent sob sporadically. She touched my hand sympathetically and ordered me another hot chocolate.

"I have to go back to work now though," I sighed.

"She'll have that to go please, Marit!" she requested, and then turned to me. "You know, men are not the be all and end all of life. Everyone gets their heart broken throughout life. Not just because of *men*, just because of human nature. Give him a chance to contact you to explain, and if he doesn't then he wasn't worth it in the first place."

I nodded and stood up to take my drink from Marit. Astrid hugged me gently and told me to text her whenever I needed to talk.

As I walked back to work, things started to look brighter already. Astrid was a star, and I mulled over my 'relationship' with Erik back at my desk. It was just one kiss. I shouldn't be so hard on myself, or on him. It wasn't like I was in the same situation as Heidi, I thought as I watched Hansen pacing his office, yelling at her on his phone. It must be horrid being married to him; I really did feel sorry for her. Who was that woman I saw him with at Marit's? I'd have to make time to investigate.

Hansen was still pacing, smoking and yelling when it was time to go home, so I just performed my usual tasks around the office and left.

The evening air was as bitter as my mood, so I picked up the pace to get home. Erik appeared from the doorway to my apartment block and smiled at me. I looked at him and frowned, unsure of the reason for his visit.

"Hey, Miss Line," he greeted me cheerily.

I nodded at him. "Erik," I coldly acknowledged his greeting.

"What happened earlier? I turned round to come and see you and you had gone, and you haven't answered my calls and messages."

I looked at my phone to find three missed calls and five text messages. "I'm sorry, it wasn't my intention to miss your calls and texts, I haven't taken my phone out of my bag all day. You seemed *busy* at the burger bar," I replied.

"Yeah, my nephew is at the difficult stage," he explained, "my sister is struggling with him at the moment. He had been good for a few days, so I decided to treat them both to food. Obviously I can't take them to the restaurant, especially as there's a three-month waiting list to go there!" he laughed.

The words 'nephew' and 'sister' lingered in the air as my brain strained to process them.

Should I confront him and check if he was telling the truth, or should I take his word for it?

"Are you ok, Line?"

"Erm, yes, sorry. I've been feeling a little off-colour today, I didn't sleep well last night."

Erik smiled. "Neither did I," he replied.

Before I had the opportunity to process any doubts that I may have, he stepped forward and kissed me. All of my doubts simply drifted away during and after the kiss.

"Should I let you get an early night tonight then?" he enquired, still smiling.

"A shot of caffeine should keep me going for a bit," I replied, shaking my head.

I invited him up to my apartment, making it clear that it was only for coffee.

The rest of the evening passed by so quickly. We chatted constantly, not having any awkward moments that couldn't be solved by drinking coffee. My phone beeped at some point to alert me that the battery was about to die, and it was then that I realised it was 2am. We said our goodbyes, with a few extra kisses on my doorstep, and I promised to keep my phone by me and respond to his messages tomorrow.

After a short, but well-rested sleep, I arose upon the third snoozing of my alarm with a smile on my face. I had decided as soon as I awoke that today was going to be a good, productive day; as soon as I had had a refreshing shower and consumed sufficient caffeine. Before either of these tasks commenced, I checked my phone for messages. Two from Astrid, asking how I was after the burger bar incident, one from Erik just wishing me a good morning. I replied to Erik's, returning the morning greeting and telling him that I would contact him during my lunch break. This message I also sent to Astrid, with the additional 'I will tell all' to her.

I sang in the shower, in the street and even in the office reception, where Aggie joined in. I was almost late, so skipped straight upstairs to my desk, carrying out the menial tasks before settling down to my 'extra-curricular' work - Kari Nordmann #14. I checked my phone for the umpteenth time and checked the status of Hansen in his office; still agitated, annoyed and pacing the room, chain-smoking his cigarettes. In the top drawer of my desk, I managed to place Kari's case folder in such a way that I could just open the drawer slightly and still be able to read any specific part of the reports without Hansen knowing. I re-read both documents but just came to the conclusion that there really was nothing I could do. They'd searched and not found any evidence, but how could I take this further? Can a suspect be charged with a serious crime, if there's no proof of a victim? How could I possibly research this to get the answers? If only I'd studied law, rather than just the secretarial course.

Hansen's office door opened, and I slammed the drawer shut, placing a couple of notepads on top of the file beforehand. I stood up so that I could look busy, but he beckoned for me to return to my desk, looking angry. Had he found out what I was up to? My mouth was dry, so I grabbed my water bottle from the desk and drained it. Hansen was standing close to me, too close. He tapped the computer.

"Can you check on the internet for cheap hotels or apartments in Asker? No hostels, but not ridiculously high prices either," he requested.

"Sure, when would you like and how long for?" I replied, breathing a sigh of relief.

"From tonight, long term. It's er, for a client," he explained.

He didn't have any clients that I was aware of, but I just smiled and clicked open the internet tab.

"Let me know when you find a couple of places for me to choose from," he said, as he returned back to his office and closed the door.

I sat and stared at the screen for a few minutes as the pages loaded.

"Internet, of course!" I stated, a little louder than I should have. 'That's how I can check these facts out!' I added, to myself this time!

Opening two tabs on the internet, I used one to literally type my questions in about the case, and the other to search for hotels for Hansen. Once I had finished, I clicked to close both search tabs and wrote Hansen's hotel details on a post-it note. My search results for the case were written down into my notebook and popped into my bag. I locked the drawer and took the note to Hansen's office. I knocked quietly as he was on the phone, and he waved me away. I stuck the note on his window and went for my lunch.

Upon my return, Hansen, obviously satisfied with the hotel results, made a swift exit around 13:00, muttering to me that he would be out of the office until further notice. I nodded as he left, but then allowed his words to sink in. 'Until further notice?', I became confused as to when he would return, and what I would do in the meantime. Would it be hours, days, months? No, surely he wouldn't leave me to my own devices for long? I continued my daily activities, and headed back down to the reception at 16:00, to collect my belongings and bid Aggie farewell.

I told the girls at our weekly meal, this time at a new Japanese restaurant, about my week's events.

"So you will have the whole office to yourself then?" Astrid commented, tentatively avoiding the flames of the chef from setting fire to her perfectly coiffured hair.

"I guess so," I mused.

"How will you get into the office? Does the receptionist have a key?" Isabella asked.

I had no idea. I assumed that Aggie would have a spare, as she was the manager of the whole building. I decided to put it to the back of my mind for now and enjoy this new restaurant experience with my wonderful friends.

7 – Hurry Home

Monday came oh so quickly, and I had mixed emotions when I awoke; the fear of the unknown, what would happen at work today, along with the joy of potentially not working with Hansen. What was most important to me was to continue to arrive on time, and hope that I could gain access to the office to collect my notes and evidence for the case.

There was a chill in the air, and I wrapped my scarf over as much of my face as possible as I walked to work. I arrived with a few minutes to spare, and could see Aggie busying herself around the reception area, so I opened the door and sat down on one of the soft, inviting chairs to the right of me. Aggie beamed at me when she saw me and trotted over with a steaming mug of sweet coffee, just how I like it. I sipped at it, but it was too hot to drink. I looked up at the clock and saw that it was time to head up to the office, so I stood up. As I was removing my hat and scarf, Aggie walked towards me, holding her hand out to indicate for me to stop.

"You aren't stopping," she whispered. I frowned, and she continued, in a very professional voice, "Mr Hansen is out of the office for the foreseeable future."

My heart leapt. Was I going to be jobless? Or paid holiday? I laughed to myself; Hansen wouldn't pay for no work!

"Mr Hansen's replacement will be here shortly." I frowned again. "Feel free to stay right here and unwrap if you wish."

Aggie raised her eyebrows and pulled a face, as a man appeared in the distance. Who could it be? As he approached, I studied him. I wasn't good with new faces, but as this was my future boss, I needed to pay full attention.

"Good morning," he nodded.

"This is MY boss, Miss Larsen," Aggie explained. "Mr Olsen."

"Good morning, Mr Olsen," I replied, still confused.

They both walked to the reception desk and discussed a few matters in hushed voices. It was unusual to hear, or not hear in this case, Aggie's voice so quiet. I continued to watch them and sipped at my coffee.

Once they had finished talking, they both approached the front door. Mr Olsen nodded at me again, and I smiled. He left, and Aggie locked the door after him. She stood and watched until he was out of view, then sat down with me.

"Sorry about that, Line," Aggie began. "We had an, erm, incident this morning. Mrs Hansen appeared when I was unlocking the door. She attacked me, ranting that I had stolen her husband."

I interrupted, "ATTACKED?? What did she do to you?"

The older woman moved her hair away from the left side of her face to reveal a great deal of redness. As she did, I saw that her hand was sore too.

"She pushed me up against the door, and I knocked my side against the handle. Then she yelled at me and slapped me." She paused as she composed herself. "She started punching me…" she continued, with a wobble in her voice.

She was interrupted by a knocking on the door, which made her jump. It was the police. She stood up to answer the door, but I stopped her, and opened it myself.

"Mrs Johnsen?" the tallest officer enquired. I gestured to Aggie.

I felt awkward as they started talking, so I stood up and wandered into the kitchen to give them some privacy. I found myself shaking as I topped up the coffee in my mug. Mrs Hansen has verbally attacked me in the past and that had left me shaken, so I sympathised with how Aggie must be feeling now. Was I shaking for my friend, or was it selfishness in fear that I may be attacked myself? Would she be waiting for me after work? I shakily retrieved my phone from my bag and started a new text for Erik.

'Hey, how are you?' it began.

He replied instantly. 'Hey, Miss U. I'm good, how are you?'

'I'm ok… Are you working today?'

'No. A lovely and relaxing day off. Are you?'

I continued to text him, explaining all that had happened already, and asked him if he would be able to walk me home after work. He of course agreed, without hesitating.

There was another knock at the front door and I almost dropped my mug as I swiftly turned to see who was there. It was paramedics, and I could see the ambulance outside with blue lights flashing. I stood in the kitchen doorway, staring as they checked her over. The building was going to be a hive of activity today, and I wondered if I should step in to take over the reception duties.

As I approached the group of people, to offer my services, I could hear Aggie refusing treatment. "No, no I will be fine. I have to work."

One of the paramedics replied, "Mrs Johnsen, you have a suspected broken wrist, we must tend to this."

As I prepared to speak, the front door opened, and Mr Olsen reappeared.

"Mrs Johnsen, Agnes, you must go to the hospital," he insisted.

"I c-can't…" she started.

"I am happy to help out, if that is of any use, Mr Olsen, Mrs Johnsen," I offered.

"Thank you, Miss Larsen, but I will be looking after the building until Mrs Johnsen is ready to return," Mr Olsen stated.

Aggie stepped towards us, "I-I can't afford to take any time from work," she explained.

My heart leapt for her.

"Agnes," Mr Olsen replied, "You can take as much time as you will need, and you will not lose ANY of your wages, I will see to it!"

At this, Aggie couldn't reply, and she allowed the paramedics to take her to the ambulance. I stood at the door and watched as the ambulance left, siren blaring.

"Morning, Line," a voice brought me back to reality with a jolt. I turned and saw Thor standing next to me.

"You made me jump, Thor! Aggie was attacked by Mr Hansen's wife, she's just been taken away in that ambulance," I pointed.

"Oh, I'm so sorry, I didn't mean to startle you," he replied.

I explained why I was so nervous and how unhinged Mrs Hansen had been in the past.

"Why don't you go home for the day?" he suggested.

"Oh, I can't. I have to wait for my new boss to arrive, but then it'll be busy, busy," I responded.

"And your new boss has just arrived!" he exclaimed, causing me to look around, and then peer through the building's window.

I looked back at Thor with confusion on my face. He was standing astride, with his thumbs pointed at his chest.

"I'm sorry, Thor, I'm a little slow today."

"That's why you should have the day off, Line," he spoke as he walked towards Mr Olsen and the desk.

Mr Olsen handed him a spare key to the office. "I will need to bill Mr Hansen for the cost of the spare key, Mr Valle," Mr Olsen explained - to Thor? Thor was my new boss?

As my brain tried to process this new piece of information, he motioned for me to follow him up to the office, via the stairs. I followed him, in a dazed manner. Using the one key, he unlocked the office door and allowed me to go in first.

"I just need to collect a few things from Mr Hansen's desk and then we can go. Collect anything that you might need for the day, like, maybe, your notes for the case?"

I nodded. "Can I check the emails please?" I asked. I needed to know if there were any updates to the case.

He smiled and nodded, disappearing into Kenneth's office and shutting the door behind him.

My hands were still shaking as I switched the computer on. I automatically turned round to grab the coffee machine before realising that I didn't need to continue with the daily tasks. I pulled out my notebooks and Kari's file and checked for emails. There were no new ones, so I shut it down again.

I looked up and Thor was waiting for me. "Are you ready to go? I will walk you home, just to be sure that you will be safe."

I felt the heat return to my face as I flushed. I nodded and we exited the office. The journey home seemed much longer than ever before, and I found myself on high alert, constantly checking around me for the threat of Heidi Hansen. Thor noticed this and placed a comforting arm around me for the remainder of the short trip home. I was sure that Heidi didn't know where I lived, but Thor still insisted on accompanying me to my apartment. And of course, I wasn't going to stop him from being close to me.

I observed as the love of my life fussed over me, sitting me onto the small sofa that I owned, and making coffee. Initially, we sat in silence as we sipped at our drinks, with Thor perched on my tiny chair. As soon as my cup was drained, he arose and refilled it. As he did so, I retrieved all of the paperwork about Kari from my bag.

"Uh-oh, no! I thought we agreed to no work, for you to have a day off," he chided me.

"This isn't just work, this is someone's life!" I replied boldly.

He stood up and I instinctively pulled the file and notebook towards me to protect it, but he was simply shifting to sit closer to me. He rested his right arm towards my back, on the back cushion, and leaned in towards me.

"Ok then, what have you got so far?"

My hands were trembling slightly as I opened up my notebook. "The suspect, who has been named Kari Nordmann due to her lack of identity, was picked up from the Melshei Forest following a caller informing the local police that she had killed someone. The caller didn't leave any other information." I looked up to Thor, for approval I suppose, and he nodded. "The local police took her in for questioning, but she wouldn't say anything. Hans… ," I paused, "Mr Hansen," I corrected, "visited her at Halden but she wouldn't speak to him. The police searched the forest for several days but couldn't find any evidence of a crime, a murder."

"Ahem," Thor responded. "So why is she in custody?" he questioned with a frown.

"Exactly!" I blurted out. "Sorry."

"Don't apologise. You are simply enthusiastic. You need passion."

"Huh?" I stumbled as he leaned forward a little.

"You need to have passion in this type of work, and you are passionate about helping 'Kari', despite Mr Hansen's disinterest."

I smiled as he leaned even closer towards me. I held my breath with excitement. My head was doing overtime, and it made me feel giddy. My stomach gurgled and he chuckled. I was mortified; my body had let me down. I had clearly become too used to the daily pastries. Thor moved back slightly, and then stood up, walking towards the kitchen area. I had put him off.

"Shall we order something for lunch?" he suggested, pulling his mobile out of his coat pocket, which had been thrown over a stool when we first arrived.

The afternoon continued as the morning had, except with a selection of comfort food and slightly less awkwardness. It was only interrupted by a phone call. It was Erik, which brought me straight back to reality.

"Are you ok?" a nervous voice asked.

I had asked him to meet me after work to walk me home!

"Oh, I am so sorry, I completely forgot. My boss walked me home this morning. We've been discussing the case all day and lost track of time."

"As long as you are ok, that's all I need to know," there was a hesitation, "Do you need rescuing?"

"What from?" I asked, standing up so that Thor couldn't eavesdrop.

"From your boss. I know you aren't keen on him, let alone confined to your home with him!"

I glanced at Thor. "I will be fine, thanks. I shall phone you later?"

"I'm working tonight," he replied.

"Ok," I replied, not knowing what to say really.

Erik would no doubt be jealous if he knew my school crush had been sitting next to me on my tiny sofa.

"OK," Erik replied. "Bye then."

"Bye," I replied, disappointed with myself for lying, for mentally cheating on him.

I returned to Thor, this time opting for the chair.

"Boyfriend?" he asked sarcastically.

"Yes," I responded cautiously.

Thor raised his eyebrows in surprise. "Oh!"

An uneasy silence filled the air. I looked down at the folder and notebook which had been placed on the table, wanting to appear busy. My temporary boss shifted uncomfortably and picked his phone up.

"I probably should be, erm, going now then," he announced.

'Please don't leave me', my inner monologue screamed out. "OK," I replied.

He stood up and slowly walked to the door. I instinctively stood up to see him out.

"See you tomorrow then, Line." Then he was gone.

8 – Crying in the Rain

I woke up with new-found ecstasy the next day, full of energy as I danced around my bedroom. 'No more loose-fitting, high-neck tops for me', I thought to myself, as I pulled out a yellow shirt, and a short, checked skirt. 'Matching underwear!', my brain exclaimed, as I stepped out of the shower. 'Makeup today, me thinks', it sang cheerily.

I literally skipped around my kitchen as I drank my coffee and made my lunch, humming to myself. I was brought back into reality by a knock at the door.

"Good morning, Miss U," Erik beamed at me.

"Erik!" I exclaimed. "I wasn't expecting you. I thought you worked late last night?"

"Yes, I did, but I couldn't let you walk to work this morning, just in case."

"Oh, thank you so much, Erik."

"How are you feeling today? You look…" he stood back a step and seemingly admire me, "stunning! Hopefully you will have no nasty visitors today, eh?!"

"Thanks," I blushed and fidgeted awkwardly, "I'm doing ok, so far," I lied.

I'd completely forgotten about Heidi actually. All I had thought of was Thor. In that moment I felt utter guilt, for not thinking about Aggie since Thor had appeared.

"You're lying!" Erik caught me out. "You don't need to put on a brave face for me. I'm here whenever you need me."

"Well, not quite 'whenever', Erik, you have a job, don't forget!"

"I don't care about my job! If you need me, I'll be there!" The guilt rose in me again.

"Stop!" He pushed a strand of hair away from my face and kissed me tenderly. "I'll do anything for you."

I swallowed loudly; my whole mouth became dry. I poured my coffee into my travel mug and grabbed my hat, scarf, coat and bag.

"Wrap up warm, Line, it is bitterly cold out there."

I smiled. "At least I work indoors," I said, as I pulled my hat on and shut the door.

We chattered like school children all the way to the office. I told him all about what had happened to Aggie, and he put a reassuring arm around my shoulders and gently pulled me close. "I'll never let anyone hurt you," he whispered, kissing me on my head, well, my hat.

"Thank you, Erik," I whispered back.

In no time we had arrived at the office, and we stopped in the doorway. Erik leaned forward and kissed me gently. I shuffled awkwardly.

"Sorry, Line, I know you don't want to be embarrassed at work," he said, pulling away from me.

He smiled, not at me, but just past my head. I turned and Aggie was standing at the door inside. She pulled a face at me and jangled her keys. We all laughed simultaneously and Aggie opened the door for me.

"I hope you are ok, Aggie?" Erik questioned her.

"Apart from this," she said, lifting her arm to show that she had a cast on.

I gasped in horror, but she just pulled a face and laughed.

"She's cool, Line, you are lucky!" Erik grinned. "I'm working tonight, but if you need me, I can come and walk you home." I nodded, and he kissed me on the cheek and watched as I safely entered the building.

"He seems very nice, Line," Aggie praised, as soon as she locked the door behind me.

"Yes, nice, Line," Thor imitated with sarcasm, as he appeared from the seating area.

I gasped, partly due to surprise, partly because he had caught me kissing Erik, and partly because he seemed to be…jealous?

His voice brought me back into the room, and I felt my face flush. "Do you have plans for tonight, Line?"

Tonight? A date?

"N…no?" It was meant to be a statement but evolved into a question.

"Excellent, we are going on a road trip!"

I looked at Aggie.

"Can I just speak to Aggie quickly?"

He nodded, "It might be worth making us drinks, do you have any flasks or travel mugs?"

"Yes," I nodded.

"Good. I shall pop out and get some snacks for us, for the journey."

I walked over to Aggie, who was now back at her desk.

"Your arm?" I blurted out.

"Correct," Aggie smirked. "What's the matter, Miss Larsen, lost for words?" She laughed and pulled a face.

"Are you ok?" I implored.

"It shook me up, Line, I won't lie. I think it has affected mentally more than physically. Mr Olsen is setting me up with a counsellor."

"Why did he make you come back to work so soon?" I questioned.

"He didn't, he said I could have as much time off as I want, paid too, but having all that time on my hands would drive me mad; too much time to think about everything.

"He has told me to keep the doors locked at all times, and he is working on some better security, with electronic features that require identity badges to gain entry. Until it is all installed, he will be staying in the building with me."

At this, Mr Olsen appeared from the kitchen with drinks for them both.

"Good morning, Miss Larsen," he smiled.

"Good morning, Mr Olsen," I responded.

Thor appeared at the door with a bag full of snacks; fruit, chocolate, bottles of water. I hadn't even made the drinks yet! I apologised and dashed to the kitchen. The coffee machine had been replenished after Mr Olsen had poured their drinks, so I grabbed a couple of travel mugs, which were stored right at the back of the cupboard and waited for it to complete the process.

"Two sugars in mine, Line," Thor said, startling me.

I realised at this moment that I was bending down in a short skirt, and stood up swiftly, automatically pulling it down at the back to cover my modesty.

I continued with the drinks and said my goodbyes to Aggie, as Thor gestured for me to follow him, which lead us to a car in the car park. It was gorgeous. I hated to be a typical girl, but all I knew was that it was red. He clicked a button on the key fob and it unlocked. I clambered gingerly into the passenger seat, ensuring that I didn't spill any of the drinks or flash too much thigh. They had safety, non-spill lids, but I didn't trust that alone, knowing how clumsy I could be at the best of times, let alone in what appeared to be a brand-new car!

"You ready?" Thor asked. I nodded, smiling.

***

The journey was long - over seven hours, to be precise. The majority of the journey was spent in an uncomfortable silence; occasionally I would glance over at my driver, then look away if he noticed, and sometimes I would catch him doing the same.

"So, this boyfriend of yours…" he left this question or statement just hanging in the uneasy air, with several hours of the journey still remaining.

I looked at him. "What about him?" I replied, simply.

"Well, tell me about him?"

"What do you want to know?"

"Stuff?"

"Ok, well he is 22, and is a host at Apparatjik."

"Where?" he questioned.

"It's a very sophisticated restaurant in Oslo," I replied, finding an unknown pride in my boyfriend.

"A host?"

"Yes, he… 'accompanies' guests to their tables and takes their orders."

"So he's a waiter, then?"

"Yes, I suppose so."

He laughed sarcastically. "En kopp te, frue?"

"What?" I quizzed.

"Cup of tea, madam?" he chortled, clearly amused by this.

I looked at him blankly.

"It's usually what waiters say to their customers, especially in England, where they all drink tea."

"OK?" I responded. This was more of a dissolution of the conversation, rather than a question.

The atmosphere became awkward again.

Our stock of food and drink depleted, we finally arrived at our destination: Melshei Forest.

"Well, this is where the report says that Kari was found, and where the caller contacted the authorities," he announced with pride. "Thought we could do a little investigating."

"Oh," I gasped.

He turned off the engine and stepped out of the car. I stayed inside for a moment, admiring his strong physique.

I had made the mistake of wearing my coat, hat and scarf on in the car, and as I stepped out, a biting gust of wind swept across me, causing me to shiver. I couldn't let my companion see my weaknesses, so I carefully shut the car door and confidently strolled over to him. He was sitting on the nearby bench, tying up some hiking boots. I looked down at my knee-high boots, with heels!

"Ready?" Thor enquired.

"Wh… Are we just going into the forest?" I asked.

He nodded. "Kari and the caller were both women, so let's see how far we can get according to how far you can go. That'll be an indicator of how far they could have been."

I didn't like the idea of this at all. His powers of deduction weren't exactly accurate, and I wasn't exactly dressed for the occasion!

Thor retrieved some knitwear from the boot of the car; a cable-knit sweater plus outerwear too and then locked the vehicle.

He strode off into the main entrance and I attempted to catch up with him.

"Come on, Line, keep up!"

He stood with his hands on his hips as I picked up speed.

"Sorry," I apologised.

The ground was uneven, and muddy at times. The air was brisk, and I pulled my hat down further to meet my scarf and protect my ears. My legs, dressed in sheer tights below my short skirt, had goosebumps. I wanted to cry with the pain of the cold, but stayed strong to save face.

"Are you still with me, Larsen?" Thor called out.

I looked up and he was the distance of a couple of trees away from me. I picked up a bit of speed, trying to look around for clues.

I didn't know what I was looking for, though. What could we find that the police couldn't find in broad daylight?

I realised that it was already getting dark.

I fumbled in my bag for my phone, to enable the torch app. I found that I had a couple of texts from Erik. I smiled. At least he wasn't an ass, like Thor was behaving!

'Miss U, Miss U xx'.

'I'm off to work now, beautiful, speak to you soon xx call me if you need me xx'.

I leaned against a tree, feeling some warmth from my blushing as I thought about Erik, and how he made me feel. I smiled as I composed a reply to the texts.

'Hey. The boss has me out on a 'field trip', so may finish late'.

I looked at the time on the clock of my phone. It was 16:00, the time I would already be leaving work!

I continued my text. 'It looks like I'll be finishing late, so I'll see you tomorrow?' I re-read it, to make sure it made sense, then clicked the send button.

'Message sending failed'.

I clicked it again and received the same error message. I had no signal amongst the depth of the forest.

I clicked on the torch app, and it lit up all around me. The trees looked like they were closing in on me. The brightness of my screen had caused the area to appear to be darker. There was an official word for that, I was sure I had learned at school, but my brain was barely functioning as I searched desperately for Thor. What were we looking for in this cold, wet forest? A body? I shivered at the thought of it, and I pulled my coat closer to me, as if it was a shield from all the bad in the world. He was nowhere in sight. I called out for him. I could hear wild animals calling out to each other, but no response from my temporary boss. I was angry that he had surged on ahead, and extremely afraid. I didn't know what animals lived in the forest. Damn! I should have paid more attention in school, rather than simply adoring Thorfinn Valle all of the time. The one time I needed him more than ever, he was nowhere. I heard twigs, maybe branches snapping all around me. What if we weren't the only humans here? What if there was a murderer out there? What if Kari wasn't the murderer and whoever was could be stalking my every move? As fear engulfed me, I felt small, cold droplets of water on my face. Were they tears or rain? They were both! I was desperately trying to not have a panic attack, fighting back my tears to put on a brave face. What was the point of protecting my pride? It wouldn't stop me from getting killed by a serial killer, or mauled to death by a grizzly bear! My breathing rate increased; my mouth was becoming dry. I had no food or drinks with me. How long would it be before someone would discover me? If the animals and murderers didn't find me, I could be in the forest for weeks. I could starve to death. I felt so small in such an imposing environment.

"En kopp te, frue?" I swung round to find Thor grinning at me, holding two hot drinks. "There's a snack van at the other entrance," he explained.

I breathed a sigh of relief, and discreetly wiped my tears and my nose with a scrunched-up tissue in my coat pocket. I managed to compose myself as I took a cup from his hand and followed him out of the forest, trying carefully not to stumble.

"Did you find anything, Line?" he asked, as he sipped his coffee.

I shook my head. "You?" I asked.

He nodded across the car park. "There's a surveillance camera up there. We should be able to get footage of Kari, and her 'victim'."

As we finished our drinks, we walked away from the car park to look for the police station. I lost track of how long we were searching for it before the boss man allowed us to return to the car. I was both angry with him for leaving me stranded and grateful for the hot drink and for his general interest in Kari's case. He had shown more interest in it than Hansen had, that was for sure.

The journey home seemed even longer than the trip to Melshei. There were twists and turns at breakneck speeds. He seemed to like the challenge of waiting until the last minute to stop, and to go faster than anyone else. I was so tired, but refused to sleep; I needed to make sure that Thor wasn't too tired to drive, and I didn't want Thor to see me asleep, he'd seen enough of my vulnerable side as far as I was concerned.

As we approached my home, I could see someone lurking in the shadows. Fear again smothered me, and I panicked internally. Thor stopped the car. I quietly thanked him and exited. He hadn't offered to walk me to my door, and part of me was glad that he didn't. However, I felt uncertain about the mysterious figure. As I walked closer, the shadow unveiled itself; it was Erik.

"Erik!" I gasped hoarsely.

"Who was that?" he asked, as the car drove away.

"It was my new boss," I replied.

Was Erik jealous, angry? I didn't know for sure, and furthermore, I didn't care – he was there for me. No sooner than the car had disappeared out of sight, I collapsed into his arms, sobbing uncontrollably.

9 - Less Than Pure

"Good morning, beautiful," a tender voice spoke to me.

I opened my eyes slowly and saw the most gorgeous blue eyes ever. It was Erik, sitting on the end of my bed, holding a mug of steaming liquid. His hair was ruffled, and his smile was sleepy. I flushed as I remembered the previous night.

Erik had helped me home, wrapped a blanket around me, heated some milk for me.

"I figured you wouldn't want caffeine at this time of night, and you look like you need warming up," he had explained, gently touching my face.

I had continued to shiver and cry for the whole duration of my soothing drink. Erik held me tenderly, but firmly, ensuring that I felt safe, stroking my damp hair.

Once the crying, and milk was depleted, he guided me to my bathroom, switching on the shower and leaving me to clean the forest off me.

The water was bliss, and warmed as well as cleansed me of the day's horrors. Once clean, I slid to the base of the shower and wept a little more, before switching off the dial and stepping out onto the bathmat. I had forgotten to grab some pyjamas out of my drawer on the way through to my bathroom, so I entered my bedroom cautiously, with a towel wrapped around me. Erik was in the living room, allowing me some privacy to dress.

I returned to the living room to find Erik sitting in the armchair. He looked up and smiled at me.

"Feeling a little better, sweetie?" he asked. I nodded and yawned. He looked at his watch. "Wow, no wonder you are yawning, it's nearly two! Come on, Line, let's get you into bed."

I gasped inwardly at the thought of Erik taking me to bed, but he did nothing more than take my hand and lead the way to my bedroom. No hidden agenda.

And now, here he was, with more comforting fluids, with the same kind look on his face.

He placed the cup on the bedside table, ignoring the clutter that was piled on it.

"I didn't want to wake you," he admitted. "It's nearly time for you to go to work, and I thought I should give you the choice of whether you want to go in or not."

"I've never *not* gone in…" I pondered. "I'd be a terrible employee to stay at home," I continued, battling a fine line between going to work or staying in bed.

"He shouldn't have put you through such an ordeal, whether he was a new boss or not," Erik stated. "Drink your tea while you think about it."

I nodded and leaned over to reach the cup. It was the best cup of tea I had ever had.

'En kopp te, frue?'. Thor's voice broke through to my thoughts, and my stomach turned. Did it affect me because it was a phrase that my crush had said? Was I feeling guilty about the mocking of Erik? Did it remind me of the previous day? Possibly all of those reasons, I concluded.

Feeling determined, I grabbed my phone from the same side table and looked at the screen. It was almost 08:00. I doubted that Thor would be there before the start of the day, so I turned my attention to Erik while I finished my tea.

"Where did you sleep last night?" I enquired.

"On the sofa," Erik replied. "Is that ok? Should I have gone home?"

"Oh, n...no, it is fine," I smiled, draining my cup.

"I'll get you a refill," Erik insisted. "That way I won't be lurking around waiting for your decision."

He returned to the kitchen, and I checked the time on my phone. 08:01 – perfect. I clicked through my contacts until I found 'Hansen' and dialled. I suddenly felt nervous, like my job was at risk, but this soon faded when a woman answered the phone.

"Good morning, Hansen and Associates," the other voice said clearly.

"Aggie?" I questioned.

"Yes," Aggie responded.

"Hey, it's Line, is Thor not in yet?"

"Thor? Oh, is that what Mr Valle's name is?" she chuckled. "Yes, he is, did you want me to try and put you through?"

"Well I'd rather talk to you, Aggie, but I do need to speak to him. I can't come in today, not feeling too good."

"Oh, that's a shame. I don't think you have had a single day off since you started, have you?"

"No. I'm wrong to take a day off, aren't I?"

"If you aren't well, then that isn't your fault – unless it's a hangover, of course..."

"No, it's not that, think I have the flu." It wasn't a total lie, I did feel very cold-like.

"Well you certainly should stay away then, I'm struggling with the broken arm – don't want to have the flu too! I'll put you through to him."

"Thanks, Aggie," I replied, feeling ashamed that again I was not paying attention to those who mattered; I hadn't given Aggie's arm a single thought since I left the office building yesterday.

As I listened to the phone ringing through to Hansen's extension, I vowed to myself to be a better friend to those who really matter.

The phone clicked; I braced myself for speaking to Thor. "Hi, Line, it's still Aggie. He's not answering the phone, I shall pass a message on?"

"Yes please, Aggie."

"Maybe he hasn't learned how to answer the phone yet, eh?!" Aggie joked. "Oh, here comes Mr Olsen, time to be professional! Thank you for your call, Miss Larsen, I shall let Mr Valle know, goodbye."

"Goodbye," I laughed.

"You've perked up a bit?" Erik smiled as he entered the room.

"Yes, Aggie, the receptionist at work, always makes me smile. Pity I can't just work with her, life would be so much better."

"Hope I can make you smile as much as she does, then," he replied, moving closer to me to set my cup down and steal a cheeky kiss.

I decided that I'd start my new resolution to treat my friends better, I kissed him back and dragged him into bed with me.

10 – Stay on these Roads

My alarm woke me up at 06:30 the next morning. Having spent the whole day in bed yesterday, I felt a little better, but found that I had been cursed with the mother of all colds. No doubt it was karma for lying about it yesterday! 'Totally worth it!', I thought to myself, as I glanced over at a very naked Erik on the other side of the bed. I felt myself blush, or was it more a glow, I wondered, as I slid over to him and kissed his curly mop of hair.

My second alarm, 'LEAVE FOR WORK', set for 07:30, beeped at me and I decided that I would have a second day off work.

"Do you need me to stay with you again today?" Erik mumbled into the pillow.

"Did you bunk off yesterday, you naughty boy?"

"No," he replied, "it was my day off, but I would have done! I'm doing the day shift every day 'til Monday now."

"Well, as much as I'd like to stay in bed 'til Monday, I think I should at least get up and make an effort today," I replied, "so I will *let* you go to work!"

"There's no need for you to get up today, listen to how snotty and gross you are. I could easily pass it on to customers, and my boss wouldn't be too happy about that!"

He paused for a second. "Damn, I have to go in, as I'm training a new girl all day. Oh, Line, I'm gutted!"

I shook my head. "It's perfectly fine, Erik. Feel free to come round after, if you want?"

"Oh, yes I will," he laughed. "I suppose I'd better pop home to get a shower and clean clothes." He sighed. "It's been truly fantastic though," he said, kissing me on the cheek.

A sudden wave of shyness rushed over me as I realised I was naked. "You go first then," I suggested, covering up and looking away.

Erik laughed and grabbed his clothes off the floor, slipping into the bathroom. I made use of this time and quickly scrambled to get my pyjamas on. I retreated to the kitchen to occupy my mind away from the naked man in my bathroom, switching the kettle on.

He emerged from the bathroom fully dressed.

"En kopp te, frue?" I blurted out my only known English phrase, which had been originally negatively aimed at his job.

"En kopp te, sir?" he corrected. "Jeg trodde du sa at du ikke kunne Engelsk?" I stared at him blankly. "I thought that you couldn't speak English?" he translated, "and clearly you don't!" He laughed. "Where did you learn that?"

"Erm…" I shifted nervously, "it must have been on tv or something?"

He smiled, declining the offer of tea or coffee.

"I shall see you later, Miss U!" He kissed me firmly on the lips, squeezing my waist to pull me close and then he was out of the door.

I called Aggie to let her know that I wouldn't be in again, and to tell Thor, and then sat in my comfy armchair with a box of tissues and my cup. I picked up my work folder to see if any of the info made more sense or not.

What had I actually achieved on Tuesday? Very little, I decided. I had got a feel for the place where the murder was alleged to have taken place. I had caught a cold, and realised what an ass Thor was! I'd learned not to underdress in winter, no matter how little time you expect to spend outdoors. Oh, and there was a surveillance camera…

I opened a new internet browser page on my phone to enable me to find out which surveillance company was stationed there, and kept my fingers crossed that it was a fully functioning one. In a few taps, I had discovered that it was JLR Surveillance Ltd, and had their phone number to contact them. I wouldn't do it today though – Erik was right, I was way too snotty and gross. I put my head back against the soft back cushion of my chair, hoping that the pounding from my head cold would cease a little.

I was jolted awake by a banging on my door. I was dizzy and my heart was racing as I stood up to see who it was. All my friends were at work, as were my family. Erik would undoubtedly be at work by now too, as my grumbling stomach confirmed. I peered through the spyhole of my door – it was Thor.

"So you aren't coming in again today then, Line?" he questioned as he pushed his way into the apartment.

"I'm not well," I sniffled.

He looked at me and grimaced. "Well, I was in the same weather conditions as you, and I'm not bunking off work!"

I stood motionless as he ranted, only moving to wipe my nose. My brain was too foggy to conjure up a retaliation. I walked back into my kitchen area and grabbed some painkillers out of my drawer. I didn't have the energy to do anything, quite frankly, so I just returned to my chair and downed the meds with my cold tea, gagging from the taste. I closed my eyes again to wait for them begin to work their magic.

I heard the tap run and opened my eyes to see Thor filing up the coffee machine.

"Want a refill?" he enquired.

My heart thawed out a little; he wasn't so bad, I guess. He settled down silently on the sofa, occasionally sipping at his drink as I continued to rest for my headache.

I awoke when Thor gently removed my cold coffee from me, before I spilled it.

"Want to go to bed?" he enquired; my heart fluttered.

He lifted me up out of my chair effortlessly and took me into my bedroom. He disappeared temporarily before returning with more painkillers, a glass of water and a fresh coffee.

"It looks like you had a rough night," he commented, "judging by the state of your bed covers."

I giggled internally as I remembered the previous night's antics, but didn't speak.

"Ok," he concluded, "get some more rest, and hopefully I'll see you back at work soon."

11 – Little Black Heart

The next few days were simply a blur, with me only surfacing when I needed fresh water or a trip to the bathroom. I was lucky to have stored plenty of medications, thanks to my Mamma.

By Sunday evening I had finally started to feel more like myself again. I emerged from my bedroom with a bundle of tissues and my glass and discovered that my mobile phone was still next to the armchair. There was also a note that had been pushed under my apartment door. As my phone's battery had been depleted over the weekend, I plugged the charger in and opened up the sheet of paper in my hand.

'Hello beautiful. I hope you are ok, I haven't been able to get to you to check. Please call me when you can – and check outside. Erik xxx'.

I smiled as I read the note, and opened up my apartment door to find a bunch of flowers precariously leaning against the door frame. I brought them indoors and found a large glass to put them into. I immediately looked at my phone to find several missed calls and messages. I scrolled down to Erik's messages, which all contained frantic messages for me, so I text back:

'So sorry Erik! Been in bed the whole time. Am awake now and feeling a little better. Xxx'.

I checked all my other messages, mainly from Isabella, and responded accordingly. While doing so, there was a tap on the door. I peered through the spyhole; it was Erik. I felt a warm glow wash over me at the thought of seeing him again, as I invited him in. He embraced me tightly.

"I've been so worried about you," he whispered into my ear.

"I'm so sorry," I replied, equally hushed.

"No, you don't need to apologise. That stupid new boss of yours is the one who should apologise. If he hadn't made you go…."

"I know," I interrupted, "It's ok."

He loosened his grip and then guided me to my sofa, pulling the blanket that rested on the back cushions onto me. I protested briefly, pointing to my phone and water glass. He returned with them swiftly, before I had the opportunity to move. He smiled at me and gently touched the end of my nose.

"Be careful of the snot," I joked.

"I don't care, I'll take everything if it is part of you."

It felt good to be out of bed, and I sneakily sat up when Erik's back was turned. I responded to all of my messages while Erik fussed around in the kitchen. I'd missed the weekly meet up with my friends, and I was gutted. They had, until now, been the highlight of my week. And I sure had plenty of news for them!

"You got here so quickly," I questioned.

"I'd just finished work, you were on my way home," he explained.

"I can stay, or go, Line, whichever you prefer," Erik offered, once I turned my attention back to him. I smiled at him, but felt awkward; I wasn't quite well enough for anything 'lively', but he seemed to sense that. "Just to keep you company, of course," he quickly added. I nodded, sipping my freshly made tea and snuggling into his chest.

I awoke several hours later in Erik's embrace, still on the sofa. Who would have thought that I could have possibly needed more sleep, but here I was! He was half-sitting and half-laying down, but looked terribly uncomfortable. I silently debated as I looked at him and simultaneously checked my phone. It was only just after 05:00.

I gently nudged Erik to wake him. "Hey, come to bed so you can be more comfortable," I suggested.

His mumbled sleepily and followed me to my room.

The next couple of hours were well rested for my companion, but for me they were restless. I felt like I was disturbing him with my fitful sleeping, so eventually decided to get up and have a refreshing shower to wash away the germs of illness.

I dressed sensibly, layered to allow for the heat of the office. Hansen had always kept the heating quite high, to encourage me to dress lightly, but I wasn't sure if Thor would know to change it. I hoped that he had no intention of any more road trips. I knew that the layers would also allow for the temperature imbalance that I was still experiencing.

This time it was my turn to leave alone. I didn't want to wake Erik up when he wasn't due to be at work for several hours, so I quietly made myself some food and drink and wrapped up warm, grabbing my coat and woollen items before gently closing my door. I would give him a wake-up call to ensure he wasn't late.

As I exited my small, enclosed street I remembered that Heidi was baying for blood and instantly regretted not waking Erik up to accompany me to work. I took a deep breath and pressed on, becoming more aware of my surrounding with every step. A usually short journey seemed never-ending today.

Eventually, I arrived at work, unharmed by anyone. The new safety system had been installed during my absence which caused me to just stand and stare, unsure of how to proceed. Aggie swiftly arrived to unlock the door for me, realising that I didn't yet have the necessary documents to gain entry otherwise.

"Larsen!" a voice boomed behind me, startling me so much that I dropped my bag, which I had been removing to speed up the disrobing process. I swung round sharply, to be confronted by Hansen. "Where the hell have you been?" he continued with his rant.

"I've been ill, Mr Hansen," I began to explain.

"These are just excuses!" he interrupted, pushing me out of the way to gain entry into the building first. "Come on, Larsen, we haven't got all day!"

I shrugged and simply stepped out of the way, throwing a quiet half-smile at Aggie, who pulled a face and made me chuckle. Hansen indicated the lift, but I just shook my head, informing him that I may still have germs.

"Ah, right, take the next one then!"

Once I was sure that the lift was on the move, I turned back to Aggie.

"How are you?" we both asked each other simultaneously.

Aggie lifted up her cast, and I showed her my bumper pack of tissues that had been shoved into my coat pocket.

"You win," I laughed. "What do I need to know about the security system?" I asked, as I removed all of my outer layers.

"Nothing right now," she responded. "Do it during work's time, not your own," she grinned.

Not sure exactly what was happening in the office, I popped my food into the fridge, and instinctively grabbed the coffee jug and headed for the stairs.

Hansen was already in his office, pacing the floor as if he'd never been away. I placed my bag into the drawer and locked it, before setting up the coffee machine.

Was he back for good, I pondered as I watched him cautiously, hoping to not catch his eye? As soon as he turned towards his door, I looked away and returned to my desk swiftly. Within seconds, he had joined me.

"So, it looks like this place cannot be run without me. The phones haven't been answered all week. No work has been done. Hiring that…that inadequate student was a grave mistake."

I didn't even dare tell him that it was this 'inadequate student' that had caused me to be off sick for most of the previous week. I didn't want him to know about my secret investigation. I didn't want to reveal my feelings for Thor. I had feelings for him? After all that had happened? I should have feelings like that for Erik, not Thor. Thor was simply a schoolgirl infatuation.

I agreed with Hansen, he had done a poor job of running the office. I wondered why the phones hadn't been answered. There were rarely any calls there anyway, so what calls had we potentially missed?

Hansen clicked his fingers. "Anybody in there?" he asked sarcastically.

I shook my head. "Sorry, Mr Hansen."

I switched on the computer and the daily chores began.

The only difference to my day today was Aggie familiarising me with the security system. I had approached her during my first trip to the reception to get Hansen's mail. I now possessed a security badge, which I would need to swipe on the machine at the outer doors to gain access.

"I have so many questions, Aggie. I've only been away a few days, but it feels like it's been years!"

"We'll get the chance to catch up, I'm sure," she replied.

My morning continued as it always does. Hansen had assured me that his wife would no longer be a concern, so I could continue to fetch the pastries and lunch. He clearly didn't wish to elaborate, but this just allowed my imagination to run wild. Before I left the building for my first trip, I unlocked my bag from my desk drawer and called Erik.

"Hello?" a sleepy Erik mumbled.

"Hey you. Are you ok? I left you to sleep for a bit before work."

"Mmmnnn.... Thanks, honey."

"I can't come there to make sure you stay awake, so you better promise me that you won't go back to sleep!" I chided playfully.

"OK, Ma'am," he responded.

"Have fun at work."

"You too."

I ended the call and headed to Marit's.

"Hey stranger!" Marit greeted me. "I've missed you."

"Sorry," I replied. "Did your profits take a massive dip?" I laughed as I collected all of Hansen's pastries.

"Yes, I have to open an hour earlier now, just to recover the loss," she joked back.

"I'd love to stop and chat, but unfortunately it is business as usual, but I'll no doubt see you very soon."

I left swiftly, still on high alert for any angry wives that may appear. Luckily, the trip was incident-free and I successfully used my new ID badge to gain entry back at work.

As I entered the office, I could see that something had been placed on my desk. A new file? a new case? I wondered.

"I need you to contact these employment agencies to look for someone to 'man' the office when I'm not here."

"OK. What do I…"

"All the information is there, Larsen," he interrupted me sharply. "I'm out for the rest of the day. Make sure you answer *all* of the calls today!" He spoke as if it was my fault alone that the calls didn't get answered when I was off.

"Now…" he continued, talking to me slowly, like I was stupid. "If my wife calls, you need to become a better liar. Act like you can actually see me. Tell her that I am in a meeting, add some hesitations, like this – 'Yes… I can see…yes… he's in his office with Mr Valle' – never say I'm in a meeting with a female. Tell her that'll I'll call her straight back. Then ring me and tell me, STRAIGHT AWAY. STRAIGHT AWAY," he repeated. "If I don't answer, send me a text message. If you have told her a specific time that I'll be out of the meeting – which I'd like you to not do – then tell me that too. All the details you tell her, you tell me. Do. You. Understand?"

I've never been an aggressive person, but I wanted to slap Hansen at this point. I simply nodded.

He finally left the office, and I was alone. I glanced at the clock; 09:45. Excellent!

I immediately retrieved my phone from my bag and rang Erik again, to ensure that he was awake. Next, I opened up the folder that Kenneth had left for me. I wasn't completely sure why it needed a whole folder for this task, as all that it contained was an A5 sheet of paper with the vague details,

'Contact all employment agencies within Oslo that supply high calibre trainee lawyers.

You need to know:

What qualifications they have

How much they cost – this is the most important detail

How soon they can start

Write each different agency's details on a separate page and leave on my desk for the morning'.

'Seems simple enough', I thought to myself, as I brought the computer back to life.

Before my work even commenced, I was interrupted by a visitor – Aggie.

"I have been asked, by Mr Hansen, to bring you your lunch, Line," she explained, handing me my pre-packed box. "As I'm just one-armed right now, I need to go do a second trip to get you a fresh jug for your coffee."

"You aren't a slave, Aggie, you have your own work to do!"

I was furious. It was his fault she had a broken arm! It was his fault I was stuck in the office, not mine and certainly not Aggie's. I explained to her my job for the day, and about my need to be in the office constantly.

"You are entitled to breaks, Line. Don't let him treat you this way! How are you supposed to have toilet breaks without being able to leave the office?"

"I daren't leave the phones, just in case Mrs Hansen calls," I responded.

"Well, just let me know if you do need to go, and I'll cover the phones," Aggie offered.

"Thanks, but…"

"No buts, do as you are told!" She pulled a face and disappeared, just to reappear with the promised jug of water.

I turned back to the computer to complete my work. As I found more information, I logged it professionally, just as Hansen had demanded. In summary, it seemed easy enough to rent, or whatever the correct term was for hiring someone on a temporary basis, and they cost around 35,000 NOK a month. WOW, that was far more than what he paid me! Sure, I wasn't a lawyer, but then neither were these, as he only wanted *trainees*, like Thor.

Once completed, I placed the file onto his desk, and then returned to my desk to start on my own work – Kari Nordmann #14.

JLR Surveillance Limited did indeed have the video for the night of the 'murder' and they would send me a copy 'straight away'.

'Straight away' turned out to be several hours, several boring hours. I had eaten my lunch slowly, drank a whole pot of coffee, some to swill down more painkillers when I could feel the remnants of my flu rage through my body. The secret pastry that was hidden in my drawer was consumed before the video came in, but when it did, the results were breathtaking.

The footage clearly showed Kari and another female, around the same age, happily entering the area, disappearing into the forest. I fast-forwarded for quite a while before Kari re-emerged, covered in blood and dirt. She took a seat on the bench that Thor and I had sat on last week, awaiting her fate. The police officers arrived 22 minutes later.

I rewatched the grainy footage a few more times but didn't spot any other clues. I paused the video that showed their arrival and increased the size. I took a screenshot, but the image was terrible. I printed it off and added it to Kari's secret file, which was still sitting in my rucksack. I forwarded the email to my personal account, along with the grainy close-up image, then deleted the original from the work account.

I had accidentally worked beyond my official hours, and Aggie reappeared to usher me out. We sat together in the reception area for a while.

"So, what have I missed?" I asked tentatively.

"Well, where to begin?" she laughed.

"I suggest last Monday."

Well, Aggie had plenty to tell me. Heidi had turned up at the office building very early, according to CCTV footage. She confronted Aggie as soon as she arrived, which escalated to the incident that had taken place when I arrived.

On Tuesday, after we left for Melshei Forest, Heidi Hansen returned, closely followed by her husband. There was a bit of a showdown in the reception area, just as the new security system was installed. She threatened Aggie, said she could cause at least twice the amount of injuries and hassles as the previous day. Hansen seemed to be able to calm her down somewhat, and managed to remove her from the building. Kenneth had rang the office several times while we were knee-deep in mud, and was fuming that there was no one there to 'represent the company'.

On Wednesday, following several more unanswered calls, Hansen phoned Thor on his personal mobile to find out what had happened. Thor took advantage of my being ill and told him that he had been too busy with work, and was of course short-staffed. Kenneth didn't seem to know whether Thor was actually busy with work or not, but 'all the calls', which equated to three – all from Heidi, checking on her husband, who still wasn't in the office – were still being diverted through to Aggie.

The new security system was installed that day too. Aggie had been provided with a specific number of security badges, and those who didn't have permission to enter weren't allowed to be able to get further than a specially cordoned section of reception, where the chairs had been moved to. Aggie was now safely behind bullet-proof glass, with just a small area to converse with visitors. Aggie had an extra supply of visitor badges, for those people who were meeting with the other clients of the building. These were issued at her discretion; if she felt threatened by anyone, she had a special number that she could ring to get a security guard to accompany her.

Mr Olsen stayed with her the whole of the week, and arranged for a restraining order, which prevented Mrs Hansen, AND Kenneth, from being within 100 metres of her. This, of course, caused issues in the building, as it was less than 100 metres.

All of this inconvenience, for 34 more other businesses located in this building, caused by one person – Hansen! So the least they could do was to make it as difficult for him in return.

On Thursday, this was put to the test. Hansen had arrived, with his wife in tow! Aggie reserved the right to refuse entrance for Heidi, and Olsen (Mr) relieved Aggie of her duties and suggested a short break, and he dealt with the Hansens. He insisted that Heidi must stay in the new reception area, and Kenneth was issued with a visitor's badge and allowed in.

The whole of the lobby was now behind this glass, and the only access for the building's tenants was to the stairs and lifts. Those with permanent security IDs could gain access to the cloakroom and kitchen, but not the visitors. Hansen spent several hours in the office, but frequently attempted to return to the lobby to satisfy his impatience. Oh, and to top up his nicotine levels.

Olsen had also had security cameras installed in every office, and had put locks on the windows to deter smokers, i.e., Hansen, from simply cracking open the window. At first, Hansen had ignored the stickers displayed around the office, informing him that no smoking was allowed, and he simply used a coffee cup with some water in. However, Olsen had also installed smoke alarms, 'to meet safety regulations', and so he was now forced to go downstairs and outside. Which, of course was very inconvenient due to the restraining order.

He called the reception phone and requested a meeting with Olsen. The latter agreed to join him in his office that afternoon. In the meantime, Kenneth paced around the office almost constantly, with the only breaks being when he was using the office phone. Thor arrived shortly before midday, using his permanent pass to get in. Lots of shouting ensued between the two alphas, right up to the point when Olsen arrived. Shunned out of Kenneth's office, it was Thor's turn to pace impatiently. Aggie, back at her desk was able to see everything, thanks to all the new monitors remotely attached to the security cameras.

The heated debate between Olsen and Hansen continued past Aggie's work hours, but she felt compelled to stay; first and foremost because she was a willing spectator, but also because she couldn't leave the reception area unattended, and of course, couldn't get too close to Mrs H. Neither party would confide in Aggie as to what was discussed, or what the outcome was, but I knew that Thor had visited me that evening after he had finished at the office. All departed around the same time, with Olsen escorting Aggie home safely.

On Friday, no one was in the office. All of Hansen's calls were automatically diverted to Aggie, which until now I hadn't known, but the building management company charged Hansen extra for this service.

I looked down at my ID badge, hanging by a clip on my trouser belt loop. It had been a hard week for Aggie, and I hadn't been there for her.

12 – How Sweet it Was

My alarm blasted out the fantastic tune that I had selected the night before. I blearily rolled over to snooze it and then rolled back, into Erik's arms. It was his day off today and I didn't want to disturb him.

Yesterday he had arrived outside my office building to ensure that I was safe walking home. He had greeted me with a kiss and we had walked back to my apartment arm in arm. The kissing had continued as soon as we were home, and through most of the night.

Now, here he was, all snuggly with an almost visible glow of contentment. I couldn't wake him up. I snuck around as quietly as possible, writing him a note to let him know where I was and to let him know there was no rush for him to leave, I would be back around 16:30.

I was glad that I had worn my warmer boots today, as there was a small dusting of snow on the floor and in the trees. I took a deep breath and could almost smell the cleanliness that I associated with snow. Looking up, I could see that the clouds were filled with snow, and I smiled – I love snow. I stood in the street and stretched my arms out wide, my gloved hands catching the occasional snowflake that fluttered down. The cold air was biting my nose, but I didn't care! It was a beautiful day; a beautiful week, in fact. Maybe even a beautiful month! I shuffled my cosy feet into the small sheet of snow that seemed to have settled on the ground.

As I arrived at the correct building, Hansen was there, smoking his cigarette. My mood dropped significantly.

"Ah, Larsen," he said, looking at his watch, which was intended as a statement gesture rather than to actually check the time, which backfired once he realised that I wasn't late; he was just impatient! "These," he continued, waving a folder, which I hoped wasn't my secret one for Kari. "Is this all the agencies that you could find?"

He meant the employment agencies. I nodded. "Did you want me to look further afield?" I asked.

"No, no, there's not really any point. They'll be even more expensive if they live further away."

I rummaged in my pocket for my new security badge, and I could feel Hansen closer to me. I looked up and saw Aggie shaking her head and pointing to him, mouthing, 'no'. He was hovering near me to gain access to the building without needing to ask Aggie. I knew it was still early so I walked past him, aiming for Marit's. I suddenly fancied a hot chocolate, to start the day right. He sighed and lit another cigarette.

I smiled to myself as I approached the small café. The queue wasn't as bad as usual, 'must be the snow', I thought to myself. I slipped indoors and ensured that the door was closed behind me.

"Ah long time, no see!" Marit announced, giving me a virtual fist bump. "I missed you, where have you been?"

"I've had the flu, I think," I replied.

I didn't mind telling work that it was definitely the flu, but to friends I admitted that it could have just been a bad cold. I knew that Hansen didn't believe that colds were as bad as they actually were.

I ordered a hot chocolate and sat at one of the tables while Marit made it. I glanced at the clock, I still had a few minutes before starting time. She brought it over to me, in a takeout cup, and sat at the next table.

"You need to come and have a longer chat sometime. You are always busy busy."

"I know, I'm sorry." I replied.

"No, I know you're busy."

"I made a pact with myself to dedicate more time to my friends rather than being all me, me, me." I was angry with myself.

"No," she replied, outreaching her hand before withdrawing it again. "Covid!" she sighed. "It's not you, I promise, no matter what you think. We are all working hard to catch up with life. We should all be allowed an extra day off a week, with no loss in pay so that we can catch up with life!"

"I don't know how that would work for you, being self-employed and the owner of this fantastic business!" I laughed.

"Yeah, I know. Maybe one day, after work or at the weekend?"

I nodded. "Yes, we will get our diaries out to book something solid in. I will be back with Hansen's pastry order shortly anyway, so I'll check my personal planner to see how busy I am." I paused and leaned forward slightly. "I have a boyfriend now," I whispered.

Marit gasped. "No way! Is it that handsome guy I saw you with the other day?"

I stopped to think a bit. I think she meant Thor? "No, I don't think… no, that was Thor, he was my crush for years." I glanced up at the clock, it was time to leave for work. "I have to go, Marit, I'm so sorry. Hansen was already outside when I passed the building just now. I can't be late, he's a nightmare."

"Ok, just hang on a sec," Marit replied, returning to her counter briefly.

She handed me one of her sheets of paper from her order book. "Here, this is my mobile number. We are friends and think we can become even better friends now?"

I nodded, and tore the paper in half, writing my number on the blank section. Standing up, I passed it to her and picked up my cup. "I'll see you soon, Marit."

A new customer entered the store, so she just waved at me. I shoved the paper into my coat pocket and briskly walked to work. Luckily Hansen had moved from the front, and so I dug out the ID and swiped it on the panel fitted to the front door. It beeped and the door opened. I looked around, but there was still no sign of him.

"He's done for the day, apparently," Aggie announced.

"Ooh, lovely," I responded, removing my hat and scarf.

"Just one message for you," she replied. "Don't miss any phone calls. Apparently he gave you specific instructions for calls from Mrs Hansen yesterday?"

"Yes, he did," I nodded.

"Well, the door is unlocked, and the office is all yours. He's told you that he will allow you to have your lunch break, but it must be in the office so that you don't miss phone calls. Mr Olsen told him that was actually illegal and he's to make other arrangements." She grinned discreetly, passing me a coffee jug full of water.

I nodded a thank you and proceeded to my office. As I opened the door, I felt a sense of freedom. I placed my hot chocolate on my desk and dropped my bag and coat on my chair. I poured the water into the coffee machine, then stopped there for a second. I wasn't even a great coffee drinker, so this probably wouldn't need to be switched on. I returned to my desk and put everything that was on my chair neatly onto the filing cabinet, retrieving Marit's phone number. I sat down in my chair and switched on the computer; mainly out of habit, but partly because I knew that Hansen could return at any moment and it took too long to switch on. And, of course, there was always a chance that I may actually find some work in my inbox.

I retrieved my comfortable work shoes and phone from my bag, which I had slung under my desk, and took the wet boots off, standing them next to the heater to dry. I added Marit's number into my contacts list and composed a message to her, explaining that I wouldn't be in for pastries today but that I'd try and pop in later. I asked when the best times for her were, and waited for the reply. I spun around in my chair and almost fell off. I laughed out loud – I didn't care!

The pc was fully functional and no, there were no emails. I thought back to what new information I had found yesterday. I had an image of Kari and another female, which I had copied from the surveillance footage – but what could I do with it? I now had two individuals that I had no information about. I wondered about what details the police would have tried to find out. I pulled my folder and notebook out of my bag and looked at my notes. They were all in a terrible state, so I sorted them into piles with the intention of rewriting them, maybe? It would certainly keep me busy. And, indeed, that is what I did.

I highlighted copies of the search documents for items of specific interest, which wasn't much. I added notes to the document according to what we encountered when Thor took me there last week, again there wasn't a lot. The initial emergency phone call hadn't been particularly useful either. I turned back to my notes for the first day, what had they done to identify Kari? There was definitely nothing on file.

I typed into a new internet browser page, 'how to identify someone from a picture'. It seemed easy enough to do: go to Google and 'drag and drop' the file. I took a deep breath. I scanned the photo of the 'victim' from the surveillance footage, and searched. The photo was too grainy; it couldn't find anything.

I sat and sipped at my hot chocolate, trying to think what I could do instead. Surely this girl should have had some kind of family? Wouldn't they be searching for her? What would they do to try and find her? They'd file a missing person's report! I thought a little more. Was there anyone looking for Kari? Had the Sandnes police bothered to check? How could I get access to it? I had to ring them for more information, although I'd be at risk of speaking to that misogynous officer. I had to put on my big girl pants and bite the bullet. I sipped a little more of my hot chocolate and mulled it over. No time like the present!

I picked up the receiver and dialled the number. A woman answered the phone, fantastic!

"Hi, I am Line from Hansen and Associates. I'm looking for more information about a case that you dealt with back in October."

"Ok, what information do you need, Line?"

"I'm wondering about whether a check was performed to find out the identity of a suspect and a victim of an alleged murder."

"Which case is this?" she replied.

"She's classed as a Kari Nordmann. She's the alleged…" I was trying to think of a professional word, "suspect. Listed as number 14." That was the best I could do.

I could hear her tapping away at her computer.

"We have no information about the victim at all, but we did run the suspect's photo and fingerprints into the database and found nothing." she explained.

"Hmm, ok, thanks for that. I have an image of the alleged victim. There was no body found, but she was seen going into the forest with Kari. Is there any way I can check? The image is too grainy to search on Google, but I think your expert hands could get further than me?" Nothing wrong with a bit of flattery to help me along.

"Well, it's a police system only, can you come by with the image?"

"I live and work in Oslo…"

"Can you send over the scanned image via email, then I can check my end?"

I exhaled a big sigh of relief. "That would be amazing! Sorry, what's your name?"

"I am Konstabel Nora Ellestad. You can send it to the email address in the file."

I breathed a big sigh of relief. "That would be great, thanks, Konstabel Ellestad!"

The call ended, and I sent over the original footage along with the screenshot I had made.

I leaned back in my chair slightly and sipped my hot chocolate until it was all gone. I became a little restless at this point. What else could I do? I wasn't sure how long it would take to run the checks, or indeed, how quickly Konstabel Ellestad would work. I faced a boring afternoon. At least I wasn't being watched all the time. I swirled around on my chair again, laughing at loud. The phone rang.

"Good…" I looked up at the clock, "…afterno-"

"Hello, Line, it's Aggie."

"Hi, Aggie. All ok?"

"Yes," she replied, "I didn't know what time you wanted to take your lunch. Oh, and I thought I'd remind you that there are cameras in every office, in case you were planning to have a party or anything?"

"Oh, blimey, I forgot about that. I bet you have had fun watching me swirling, eh?"

Aggie laughed. "Oh yes, has certainly kept me entertained."

I felt myself blush. "I can go for lunch whenever it suits you, Aggie. I have food in my bag, so it would just be a drink or toilet break at most."

"Have you finished your coffee already?"

I looked over at the machine. "Actually, no. I had a hot chocolate, but not started on the coffee yet. Don't really fancy it. I fancy tea."

"Ah, leave it with me!" she replied, ending the call.

Within minutes she appeared in the office, with a box of assorted teabags and some small milk cartons carried under her one working arm.

"You can either put some tea in the machine instead of the coffee, or just run the water through without anything and use the teabags in your cup. Your choice."

"Oh thank you so much, Aggie. I'll prob just use the water, that way I can choose which tea I want. Take a seat, if you wanted to stop?"

"I have a few minutes spare, just for you, Line."

"Excellent," I replied. "Do you want one?"

"Oh, no thank you, I have been swimming in it since Mr Olsen has been here. He's been fussing over me since the 'H' incident!"

"Good! You need to feel safe; you need to BE safe!"

"It's a bit difficult not to be right now, with all the windows. I'd only just got used to all the Covid safety updates, now I just feel like a goldfish."

I nodded. "Yes, I can see that you feel a little more, visible, I guess. But if you think about it, with the security system in place now, you get a notification when someone enters the building. So you can potter around more, rather than being glued to the desk all the time."

"Ah, yes. I never really thought about that. That is, of course, assuming that Mr Olsen ever leaves!"

"Is there a reason that he's still here, despite all the safety features being done?"

"Mr Hansen," she replied simply. I looked swiftly at the door. "No, he's not here, silly. Mr Olsen doesn't want me here alone while Mr Hansen is still around."

"But he works here, he's rented an office?"

"Yes. Mr Olsen has told him that he needs to either find an alternative office or get someone else in, like a manager."

"A new manager would be lovely, but I can't see him being able to afford someone else. He asked me to research some employment agencies to find another manager, but the rates are incredible!"

"Not good for someone who can't even afford the office bills at times. And we are quite cheap!" she pulled a face. "I probably shouldn't say things like that!" she chided herself.

I leaned forward slightly. "Is it just visual cameras here, or do they have sound too?" I asked.

"Just visual," she replied, "so don't worry about the singing."

"Phew! That's a relief!" I laughed.

We sat and chatted for a while, and Aggie looked after the office while I nipped to the toilet, and then she had to get back to her desk.

"Show him that you are ok without him!" I told her, as she left.

I chose a regular, caffeine teabag, and topped up my cup with water.

"En kopp te, frue?" I muttered to myself, smiling as I thought of Erik, hair ruffled, in bed this morning.

I looked at my phone and found a message from him.

'Good morning beautiful. Just woke up - you should have woken me. It's snowing pretty hard now'.

I stood back up and walked to the window. The whole city appeared to be covered in a white blanket. I was so glad that I didn't drive, it looked like a nightmare out there.

I spent the afternoon munching on my lunch and texting Erik. I had also made a point of getting in contact with all of my friends. We were so used to meeting up on Fridays that I had let things slide.

"New me, new life!" I mumbled to myself, as I clicked 'send' on the last of the messages. I'd made a point of not sending one group message to all of them, it had to be more personalised to be authentic. It took longer, but I wasn't exactly short of time!

I walked back to the window. I wanted to be out there, in the lovely snow. I walked back to the desk again. I wasn't sure if I could live this sort of life anymore. Everything else was perfect, though, it was only work that made me dissatisfied. Plenty of people had boring jobs too, I guess. I swirled around on my chair a few times until it was time to go home.

13 - White Canvas

It has been another fantastic night with Erik last night. He had popped home while I was at work, to get some clean clothes and some ingredients so that he could make us dinner later. I had already asked if he wanted to stay the night - he hadn't wanted to assume that it was a given before then. I let him know that I was meeting Marit after work, just to catch up on life, so he said he would meet me at my apartment later on that evening.

Marit was surprisingly friendly and understandable. She sat quietly and listened to all of my recent news, not judging any of it. She seemed wise beyond her years - there was probably a background story there, and I had no doubt that one day she would open up to me the way I had done to her. My tummy rumbled at some point, and Marit shared a couple of pastries that were remaining from the day's sales - probably because Hansen hadn't had any! I offered to pay, but she waved me away.

Soon it was dark and I remembered that I still needed to get home. Marit was lucky on that score as she lived above the café. She unlocked the door for me and watched and waited until I disappeared from view.

When I arrived at my apartment, Erik was sitting outside, shivering. My heart warmed for him and I apologised profusely. 'Should I give him a key?' I thought to myself. No, it was too soon, I didn't want to appear too keen.

The meal that Erik cooked for us was tremendous; steak and salad. I'd always had my steak well-done on the odd occasion that we were treated to it at home, but Erik cooked this to a medium, and it was lovely and tender. After dinner, we sat together on the sofa to watch some tv, and fell asleep, right there.

***

Now it was morning, and time to face another day at work. Still shy of my body in daylight, I got undressed in my bedroom, peeping out of my window to check the weather. There was a lot more snow now, so I chose some clothes suitable for the cold, layering again to cover all bases.

I saw a flash of lightning from the window, so ran back to see if there was more to come. There was no thunder, and the couple of extra flashes of lightning seemed quite a long way away; it almost looked like the flash I saw was a reflection on the building opposite my apartment block. I'd never really known storms during snow weather, but anything could happen lately - weather around the globe was generally unpredictable and unstable.

The water of the shower was just the right temperature and I found myself singing. Suddenly I heard singing behind me, and I found Erik stepping into the shower with me. This was truly the best shower of my life!

The repercussions of the shower had caused me to fall behind with my routine, but it was definitely worth it. I dressed swiftly and grabbed a quick coffee from the machine, kissing a very naked Erik goodbye.

"Don't forget I'm on the nightshift for the next few days," he reminded me.

This made me feel sad, but at the same time, I didn't want to be… in each other's pockets, I think the phrase is.

"Ok, you are welcome to stay here as long as you need to be," I replied, kissing him again and rushing out of the front door.

I hurriedly walked to work, which was rather difficult with so much snow, but I did my best. I arrived at the building right on time. I swiped my ID at the door, waved and said hi to Aggie, then dashed up the stairs to the office. As I approached, I realised that the door was probably locked, and if that was the case, no one was probably checking on my attendance times. At the door, I found it was unlocked, so I walked in and put the lights on. I peered into Hansen's office, but there was no sign of life, so it looked like I was on my own again today.

I placed my bag in my drawer and locked it - just in case - and collected the jug for the coffee machine. I switched on my computer, leaving it to load up while I filled the jug. I trotted down the stairs, still in my outer clothes, and de-robed them as I waited for the kettle to finish boiling, which I correctly assumed that Aggie had switched on moments ago.

"Hello, Line, you were pushing it a bit today, weren't you?" she laughed as she walked in to join me.

"Yes, I think that's been my worst lateness ever!" I exclaimed, truly disappointed in myself. "The office was unlocked when I came in," I continued, "has Hansen been in?"

"No," she replied, "I have permission to lock and unlock it for you. Unfortunately, he hasn't given permission for you to have the key."

"That doesn't surprise me in the slightest! I'm the only constant there right now, but still the underdog!"

"Sometimes it can be a good thing to stay under the radar, Line," she suggested wisely.

I replied, with a "Hmmmm...," and grabbed a cup from the cupboard.

She sat down at the table, and I filled up the jug with water from the tap and made myself a tea.

"I'd better get back to my so busy day," I laughed. "Can you let me know if any visitors check in for me?"

"Sure will," she saluted me.

I smiled, and left her to carry on with whatever task she had set out to do.

Back in the office, I found that I had a response from the Konstabel.

I sat down with my mug and clicked the email to open it. While it loaded, I put on my work boots and poured the water from the jug into the coffee machine.

The email read:

'Hello, Line. I have looked at the images that you have sent to me. They are quite poor copies, but it looks like we have a couple of matches. I have attached photos of the two women that matched so far.

HANNA SVENSDOTTER

Hanna, aged 15 was reported missing on 14th May 2018 by her parents, Birgit and Oskar, and no sign of her has been seen since that date.

FREYA BERGEN

Freya was 16 when she was reported missing in August 2019. She had no family, and was reported missing by a neighbour. Apparently she had been evicted from her home.

I hope that this helps.'

I hoped that it would help too! I clicked to open the attachments. They both contained an image along with descriptions of the disappearances. I couldn't see anything of use at this time, so printed them both and placed them into Kari's folder. I forwarded the email to my personal one and then deleted the original – you've got to cover your tracks!

The rest of the day went slowly, with nothing really happening at all. There was the occasional hoax call, which was probably Hansen to check if I was there and answering the phone!

I left the office right on time today; Hansen wasn't getting any extra time off me! I sat and chatted to Aggie for a few minutes. There was no Mr Olsen in the vicinity anymore. He had agreed to give her some space to keep working, as all the breaks he was allowing her were just giving her more time to think. His one condition was that he have an intercom system and a CCTV camera set up outside so that no one could enter without her knowledge and approval. She was more than happy with that, and it was going to happen tomorrow. I felt relieved for her, it had been a tough time, very traumatic and now there was a light at the end of that tunnel.

"I know it's a little late for the gesture, but I am happy to walk you home, if you'd like?"

"You are so kind, Line. I catch the bus just outside here," she pointed outside, "she never has the opportunity."

I changed my shoes and put on my extra layers - ready for the season's battering.

"I hope you are right, Aggie, I don't want anything bad to happen. Anything else, I guess. Did you want me to wait with you until you catch the bus?"

"No, it's fine, you get on home to your sweetheart," she laughed, pulling a face.

"Oh, he's working nights until Sunday, so I'll be home alone."

"Enjoy the peace then," she said, bulldozing me out of the door and locking it behind her.

I headed towards Marit's just as she was closing up. She waved me in. She prepared a couple of hot chocolates and brought them to a nearby table. I sat down and smiled at her.

"You are too kind, Marit," I told her.

"It's nothing, really," she replied dismissively.

We drank, and chatted about so many things, and realised that we had more in common than we thought.

It was dark again when we decided to leave. Marit placed the dirty pots into the dishwasher and switched it on while I put my outer clothes on. At the door, she turned all the lights off and locked up.

The snow had started to dissipate, much to my disappointment, and I made a slow journey home, shuffling my feet in what was left of the mush on the ground.

14 – Riding the Crest

A boring day lay ahead of me when I woke this morning, rather similar to the previously boring night. Well, that was unfair to say, really. After my text messages to the girls the other day, I'd managed to speak to Isabella, in the hope of catching up on all the gossip, but there was none. I wasn't going to just blurt out everything that had happened with me, it wasn't fair to bombard them with all of my woes. We had, however, managed to secure our Friday night arrangements for this week – I'd only missed one Friday and was looking forward to it!

I had been so spoiled by Erik, I guess, and now he was back at work, I felt lonely. I'd padded round my home most of the evening, like a wild animal in a cage, finally deciding on an early night.

I woke up early, most likely due to the early night. I didn't want to go to work early, there was just no need to extend the length of an already slow workday. I huffed as I switched my phone on. I had missed a message from Erik last night after he had finished work. Was it too early to reply? I glanced over at the clock on my cooker: 06:22. Yes, it was! He no doubt would still be in bed, so I set an alarm on my phone to call him on my lunch break.

I cooked myself a breakfast of mackerel, which I found at the very back of my freezer, and scrambled egg, and at the same time I cooked some pasta for my lunch – no doubt I wouldn't be able to get out of the office. I had some pesto in the cupboard that I could eat it with, and there was some chicken leftover from a dinner that we had the other night. Leftover salad from our steak night was added to it, and once I had eaten my breakfast, I felt satisfied on all fronts.

Rather than just visiting Marit after work and blagging free drinks and pastries, I decided to make more of an effort to help her keep her business thriving. It had been a rough couple of years, due to

Covid and it was only with financial help from family and the government that she was able to re-open. I would continue to do my best to contribute. I looked down at my lunch – I should have probably thought of that sooner; another mental note to *not* make lunch after all!

I found an old travel mug which read, 'Today is your day!'; it was grubby and old, but it would have to do, for now. I gave it a quick wash and then I was ready to roll.

The cafe was quite busy when I arrived, and I realised that maybe this impromptu visit was not such a good idea. I joined the end of the queue, which was outside. I spent nearly the whole queuing time regretting the choice, and maybe today wasn't my day! However, it was still too early for work, so I persevered. I glanced over at a shop a few doors down from Marit's and saw travel brochures. I made a mental note to grab one or two on the way to work, to break up my day a little.

Finally, it was my turn to buy my drink. Marit had some travel mugs with 'You Are Enough' emblazoned on them. That would do nicely. I pointed to one when I placed my order – extra-large hot chocolate. I'd have to start having extra exercise to burn off all of these naughty drinks that I was indulging in lately!

The original plan was to sit at a table, but found them all occupied, so I waved to my new friend and headed out of the stuffy space. True to my word, I grabbed a couple of travel brochures and slipped them into my bag. Further along, I found a quaint little book shop. It was shut right now but would be open at lunchtime if I could manage to get out. I didn't really have many books at home, maybe now was the perfect time to pick up the perfect page turner.

I reluctantly shuffled to work, my boots catching the last of the slushy, grey snow. I fumbled about in my pocket for my ID badge, but Aggie saw my struggle and dashed to open the door for me. She pulled a face at me, and I smiled; a mere funny face could easily lift a mood.

"You're not meant to let me in," I scolded her, wagging a finger in jest.

"Good morning to you too, Line," she replied, grabbing the travel brochures from under my arm, before they could slide away on the newly cleaned floor. "Are you going on holiday?" she asked.

I raised my eyebrows, "Not on the wages I get from here!" I laughed. "It's just a little light reading to relieve the tedium of my day."

Aggie smiled sympathetically; I think it was the first time I'd seen her not pull a face to cheer me up.

"Can I grab the mail too please, saves me doing an extra trip, I suppose."

Aggie handed me a couple of letters for Hansen. I returned to the office, humming to myself, and placed the letters on my boss' desk.

I returned to my desk and swirled around in my seat. I took my folder, notebook and phone out of my bag and popped them into my drawer. I moved the other items into my small drawer, which I always used in case I needed to slide it shut quickly. I switched my pc on, and swirled in my chair until it beeped for the password to my emails. I typed it in and watched it load. I then clicked another tab on my internet browser and searched for social media platforms. My plan today, between drink breaks, lunch and holiday brochures, was to see if I could find the two girls who were possibly connected to the surveillance footage I was researching: Hanna and Freya.

I had decided this route for several reasons; to find out about them and their lives, see if I could find out why they would go missing and to see if there was a link to Kari.

As there were no outstanding emails, I pressed on with my search. There were 18 Hanna Svensdotters, which surprised me. Only two had a profile picture of themselves, or at least that was what I assumed. She was only 15 when she went missing, but I knew only too well how grown up a 15-year-old girl could look when she wanted to. I clicked each account in turn and looked through her photos.

Hanna #1 had a bio stating that she was from Trondheim. She seemed to have a huge amount of friends, and they didn't seem to be just online friends; there were hundreds of photos with her 'bitches' (her words, not mine!). There was nothing on there about her being missing; there were multiple posts and photos a day.

I decided not to find out all the info about each girl/woman and focus on how old they were, how recently they had posted and whether there was any information about her being missing.

My research was interrupted at approximately 09:38 by a phone call. It was Heidi Hansen. What had Hansen asked me to do? Act as if I can see him and see how busy he is in his office, and say he'll call back as soon as possible.

"Hello, Mrs Hansen. Mr Hansen is just… he's just on his way to the phone now… oh, he's just answered a call on that phone. I've indicated that you are on the other line and he's just held up a finger to say he'll just be a minute. Did you want me to get him to call you back?"

"No, I'll wait."

Damn, how was I going to get out of this one? This woman was relentless. Ah, I could ring him from his work phone to tell him she's holding and ask for advice. I dashed into his office with the post-it note that I kept his number on, and rang him. He answered after a couple of rings. "Larsen, what?"

"Mr Hansen," I remained polite despite the dislike I felt for him. "Your wife is on the other line and won't give up. I've told her you're just on a call on this phone, but she's holding."

"Ok, Larsen, I shall call her now."

Hopefully she would automatically disconnect my phone line when she answered his call? Yes, I was right. Back to my hot chocolate and research.

The majority of the Hannas were young, but they all seemed to still be active on the social media platforms. I just had a couple left to check, when I received another call.

"Not Heidi again, I hope," I said under my breath, as I reached to lift the receiver.

"Good morning, Han-."

"Line, It's Aggie. There's a gentleman here to meet Mr Hansen. Apparently, he has an appointment to meet him at 10:00?"

"Erm… I'm not aware of any meeting but will come down to see him."

I made sure that I closed down the social media search, for now, and locked all my drawers, slipping my phone into my trouser pocket.

As I approached Aggie's desk to get the name of the person waiting, Hansen appeared at the main entrance. The buzzer startled Aggie, and Hansen's gruff voice insisted on entering. Aggie reluctantly agreed, knowing that he couldn't get anywhere other than the new reception area. He gestured impatiently for me to go and see him.

"I'm holding some interviews today for the management job. Here's an itinerary of the times and names. I want you here before the interview starts to offer a hot drink or water to the interviewee." He waved a sheet of paper in front of me.

I nodded. "Where will the interviews be held?" I asked.

"He looked at me with distaste. "Here," he waved his bony, wrinkled hand at the reception area, and I automatically raised my eyebrows in surprise. He spotted this and confronted me.

"Got a problem with that, Larsen?"

I shook my head and approached the man. Glancing at the list, I saw that the first person was Sven Hagen.

"Sven," I addressed the smartly dressed man.

He looked up at me and smiled. A pang of pity made my stomach lurch slightly, a bit like when you watch a horror movie and you knew someone was going to be killed.

I smiled back. "Would you like a drink?" I asked politely. He declined.

"That'll be all, Larsen," Hansen dismissed me.

I returned to the office with the piece of paper.

I excitedly texted Isabella.

'I hv work! Kenneth is interviewing for manager job!'

I looked at the slip of paper. They were scheduled every hour.

The phone rang – it was Mrs Hansen again. I had no idea what he had told her, but at least I had a little nugget of truth to guide me.

"Mrs Hansen, good morning, how are-"

"Put me through to my husband!"

"He's just in a-"

"No, he's not, I just spoke to him."

"A gentleman, Sven, arrived just now for an interview with him. A very nice young man, very handsome. It would be lovely to have him work in the office." I kept up the dialogue in an attempt to stop her from getting irate. "I believe there is a spare-"

"But he's not allowed in the office anymore?"

"No, I know, he is in the lobby. I just offered him a drink, but he declined. Looking at the schedule of interviews, he's busy all day, but he may have a little time between interviews if you need him urgently?"

"No, it's fine," she replied, and hung up.

It felt like a victory to me.

Aggie rang me as soon as any interviewee appeared in the lobby, to allow me to offer him a drink before the interview started. No, I wasn't just assuming gender, all the interviewees were male!

As a dutiful employee, I managed to successfully approach each person and offer drinks before Hansen arrived. Where he was in between interviews, I had no idea.

When I was handing a drink to the 14:00 interviewee, Jakob, I caught a glimpse of Heidi hovering outside. It looked like she wasn't just waiting for her husband, she was also checking if the interviews were real. As far as I was concerned, it was one step closer to gaining her trust, which would make future phone calls easier for me.

In the interim, I conducted a check of each of the other Hannas. I was close to the last of them when I found the missing person. There were dozens of posts to her 'wall' asking for her to contact various friends and family. I looked at her photos to see if I could find a recent one to crossmatch the grainy surveillance footage. The most recent one was just last week. I looked through my notes; the alleged murder had taken place at the beginning of October.

Surely this meant that it was Freya? Well, I wasn't going to jump to conclusions, I would have to do an equally thorough search for her too. It looked like this was a job for tomorrow. I switched everything off and left the office. Downstairs, Aggie was still there, as was Hansen with his last interviewee. He looked at his watch, ready the admonish me for leaving early, but instead, he raised his eyebrows, and returned his attention to the young man he was with.

It was snowing again outside, but I was dressed for it. I trudged through the settling snow at my feet, to head to the book shop for a browse. I found a couple of great crime books – staying close to my roots, the reason why I decided on a career in law.

Back in my apartment, I spoke to Isabella on the phone as I cooked my dinner.

"I had such a great, full-on day!" I told her. "It really makes the difference to have actual work to do."

"I'm so happy for you, let's hope it continues!"

She told me about her day at work; she was unfortunate to also be treated like a general dogsbody, attending to hot drinks and changing the paper in the copy machine.

"Well that's a step up," I sympathised.

"Not when it is just every few weeks!"

It was indeed the same for the both of us.

We continued our evenings alone, happy in the knowledge that we would see each other the next evening.

I text Erik to see how he was doing. I'd been so busy that I hadn't noticed the time, and just worked at my desk, grazing on my pesto chicken pasta salad.

Sleep started creeping up on me early, and I found my eyes drooping when I started reading my book. I decided to continue to read it in bed, but barely got past two pages.

15 – A Little Bit

I had again missed the opportunity to speak to Erik the previous night, I discovered when I looked at my phone messages.

'Hey Miss U. You up for a visitor? I've just finished now.'

I looked at the time of the message: 23:04. Damn! I had fallen asleep at around 10.

It was another early morning, and as I was expecting a later evening, I snuggled back under the covers, to try and sleep a little longer.

My 'last chance' alarm startled me at 07:30, and I jumped out of bed and rushed to get ready for work. It was definitely going to be a coffee day today.

The office seemed quiet, although Aggie was doing an extra clean of the reception area following the meetings yesterday; they had overrun last night and Aggie had left them to it. There had been an abundance of cups to collect and wash, and bits of paper and staples strewn on the floor. Hansen really was obnoxious!

I offered to help her, but she waved me away, telling me that I should get to my office. I wasn't sure if she was angry or not, but there had been no funny face. I ignored her dismissal and started to collect the last remaining cups.

"It's my boss' mess and you only have one arm," I insisted.

In the kitchen, I removed all of my outerwear and started washing up the cups. Aggie arrived with the last of the cups and shooed me away, this time pulling a face. Confident that she was ok, I filled up the coffee pot and walked upstairs to the office. The door had been unlocked, thanks to Aggie – she really was a star.

As there was no sign of Hansen or a new manager, I knew the day would be slower. I searched for Freya Bergens on social media, refilling my coffee cup regularly. I looked up at the clock and it was moving on a bit, so it wouldn't be long before it was lunchtime. I didn't want too much to eat, or it would spoil my appetite. I closed down the social media tab on my computer and grabbed my bag, leaving for a trip to Marit's, letting Aggie know that the office phone needed to be monitored.

As expected, the coffee shop was busy, and the queue was long, but I pressed on. Out of the corner of my eye, I spotted Hansen with an unknown woman. I was sure it was the same woman that I had seen him with a few weeks ago. I covered some more of my face, so that he wouldn't recognise me, peering around it occasionally. Soon it was my turn to be served. Marit bagged up a couple of pastries and refilled my 'You Are Enough' with luscious hot chocolate. I found a table at the other end of the café, retrieved my phone and threw my bag and coat on the chair next to me.

I sent a text to Erik, to see if he was awake, which he was.

'I'm currently doing a covert op, but will call you in about 15 minutes, if you are free?'.

'Always free for you, gorgeous'.

I smiled. I had never really been called gorgeous or beautiful, and it was quite alien to me. I knew I wasn't. I'd been unfortunate to be an ugly baby and child, and had no doubt that I hadn't improved with age, but it warmed me up when he called it me.

I spotted Hansen rise out of his chair, and so did the woman. He exited the café, holding the door open for the woman like a true gentleman, and I watched them walk in the opposite direction to the office building. I looked at the time on my phone and left the café, waving to Marit.

I retrieved my phone from my coat pocket and phoned Erik. "Hey, Miss U," he greeted me.

"Hey, yourself."

"I've missed you this week," he admitted, "I can't wait to see you again."

"When is your next day off?" I enquired.

"Monday," he responded.

"Come round after I've finished work and stay over?" I replied, unsure if this was a suggestion or request.

"Most definitely!" he exclaimed.

I was back at the building, so we said our goodbyes and I swiped myself in with my ID card. Finally, I was making progress with the security.

The afternoon breezed by, with multiple text message conversations with Erik, Isabella, Astrid, Marit and even Helene. The girls finished early on Fridays and were all at home getting ready for meeting up. In my rush, I had failed to pack my clothes and makeup to get ready at work, so would have to go home. At least this meant I could have a shower, seeing as I'd missed one this morning.

I continued to examine social media for Freya Bergens. At just before 16:00 I spotted one that looked remarkably like both the footage and the photo that Konstabel Ellestad had sent me. There wasn't, however, much information on her profile to show that she was missing. Why would nobody out there want to find her? Did she have no family or friends? Her profile did seem to be rather barren.

It was time to leave, so I packed up all of my belongings, emptied the coffee filter and pulled the coffee jug off the machine. Downstairs, Aggie was busy cleaning.

"Are you leaving early today, Aggie?"

I knew that she was always the last one to leave, much later than me.

"Yes, it's my wedding anniversary today, so it is date night!"

"Ooh, how exciting!" I replied. "Let me finish up for you?" I suggested.

"No, no, I'm done now."

We both left the building at the same time.

"See you on Monday," I said. She nodded.

As I watched her walk to the bus stop, I saw a figure to the left of me. I tried not to go into panic-mode, and was relieved when I saw that it was Erik.

He embraced me and I felt happiness again.

"I thought you had to work?" I probed.

"Yes, I'm going there now, just wanted to see you," he explained.

He hugged me again and kissed me on the lips. "I don't want to leave you now," he mumbled into my coat.

"Come round after work, I will ensure that I stay awake. Then we can spend some of the day together," I suggested.

"Mmm, yes, are you sure?" he replied.

"100% sure!" I replied.

He hugged me for just a minute more and then he left for work. I dreamily embarked on my trip home and got ready for the night out.

***

The 'Friday Buffet' was amazing, and I gorged on pizza. I'd had excess pasta all week so that didn't appeal to me. The wine flowed, and the conversation was constant.

I told them about all that had happened since I'd last seen them; Melshei Forest, Aggie and Heidi, Thor and Erik. There was a wide variety of responses.

"Wasn't Thor your crush?" "Are you dating both of them?" "How could someone leave you alone in a dark forest? What kind of man is he?" "Erik sounds amazing, don't let him go!" "You need to learn some kind of martial arts, so you can defend yourself more!"

This last statement started a whole new discussion. Apparently, we were going to find somewhere and train every week. Helene had been working with a Sensei, which was like a master of judo or something, she was working on a logo for his new classes, and she promised to speak to him next week. This caused a flurry of emotions amongst the group; it was something healthier for us to do, and it meant that we could spend more time with each other. A win-win situation.

Astrid had nothing of interest to report. Isabella had copywritten a report on salmon, giving her boss the credit, as always. She had taken an interest in photography recently too, taking shots of the fisherman she had encountered during her research.

"Show us?" I pleaded.

She shook her head. "It's much too boring for you all, especially tonight!"

The others agreed and laughed.

"Well, we will have to meet up after work one afternoon and show me then," I pressed further.

As I stood up to get another helping of pizza, along with a token bit of salad, I almost bumped into someone. It was Aggie.

"Hello, stranger!" she announced.

"Wh…what are you doing here?" I asked.

"Anders has paid for a meal out as a special treat for our anniversary."

"Excellent!" I exclaimed, angry with myself for not remembering this information, which had only been shared with me a couple of hours ago.

I was determined to focus more on my friends. I made a point of going to their table to speak to them both for a few minutes. Anders Johnsen was a really lovely man, although very shy.

As we made to leave for the night, I paid for the Johnsens to have an extra bottle of wine. We, the girls that is, all departed together then went in our own directions. I knew that I'd be seeing Erik fairly soon.

16 – Nothing is Keeping you Here

I sat patiently, waiting for Erik to arrive. The expected time came and went. I found myself pacing and peering out of my apartment window, looking for him. The fuzzy, warm feeling that I had was dying down, and I sat down on my sofa, staring absentmindedly at my phone. He would have called me if he couldn't make it, wouldn't he?

'I mustn't fall asleep', I thought to myself. I made myself a pot of coffee, to wake me up a bit. I walked back over to the window with my cup of coffee; I still couldn't see him.

Suddenly, there was a quiet knock at the door. "Erik!" I gasped to myself.

I rushed to the door to find Erik with a bag full of snacks and some bottles of beer. I hugged him.

"Thought I should grab some supplies first. I've brought myself some spare clothes too – I hope you don't mind?"

"No, not at all. I'm just glad you are here!"

We sat together on my little sofa, listening to music on my phone, drinking beer. I wasn't hungry enough to eat the snacks, though, and neither was Erik, as he had eaten at work. They'd keep for the weekend.

We spent the whole weekend doing very little. Erik still had work during the evenings, but knowing he was coming back pleased me. We slept, we ate, we drank, we kissed.

***

Monday came around too quickly. I didn't want to leave the warm safety of my home, but I had to earn a living.

I left Erik asleep in my bed. That was the hardest part. Sure, he'd still be there when I came home, and I still had the whole night with him, but still… I knew where I'd rather be. I showered and dressed silently, not wanting to wake him up.

I surveyed the contents of the fridge to throw together some lunch. All that we, erm, well, *I*, had on hand was some bread, salad and snack remnants. Although I wasn't sure what work would be like today, my lunch break in particular, I couldn't leave Erik here with no food, so I left it all as was. I grabbed my notebook out of my bag to write him a note.

I looked at the book. I hadn't thought about work; Kari, Freya… at all.

I continued with the note. 'I should probably leave him a key', I thought, 'but I don't want him to think that he has a key to use all the time'. I mulled it over for a few minutes.

'Erik, I've left you with some snacks from the weekend. If you need to go anywhere, you can borrow my spare key, which is on the hook in the plates cupboard. XXX'.

That wasn't too bad. Knowing it was a spare key would stop him from thinking I was *giving* it to him?

I swung my coat on and left.

There was no time to hesitate during the walk, I was running late! I arrived at the building and swiped my ID card. Aggie was fussing around watering her plants. I didn't want to scare her, as she had been through enough recently, so I just said hi, and voyaged to the kitchen and cloakroom.

"I'm running a little late, Aggie, but will come and see you as soon as possible," I shouted to her, waving when she looked at me.

I filled the coffee jug with water and walked upstairs to the office. No one was inside, so I just dumped my bag on the desk and filled up the coffee machine. I switched on my computer and waited for it to load up.

I realised that I was again at a loose end. I may have discovered who Kari's *alleged* victim was, but that didn't mean that I knew how to find her - dead or alive! I sat and stared at my computer screen, feeling deflated. I didn't even feel like swirling around in my chair today. All I could think of was a naked Erik at home right now, while I was sitting here with nothing to do!

A call came in, but it was just Aggie.

"Hi, Line, you have a new manager joining you soon. He'll be here shortly, according to a delightful email that Mr Hansen sent to us over the weekend. Brace yourself, eh?!"

I could almost hear the face-pulling. "Oh, and thank you for the wine on Friday night, it was a lovely treat."

"Not a problem, hope you had a good anniversary," I replied.

A new manager… I wondered which one it would be. I remembered that I'd been polite and professional with all of them, so hadn't got off to a poor start, hopefully. I ensured that all of my notes about the case were secured, away from prying eyes. I fussed around a little, feeling nervous. There was nothing to clean as that was sorted out when the office was vacant. The coffee was on. There were clean cups. There was nothing else for me to do.

"Hello, Larsen," a voice interrupted my thoughts.

I looked up, stunned. It was Thor.

"Thor? H- how?"

"I guess he decided that I was the best for the job, Line."

He poured himself a coffee and sat at the desk in Hansen's office. I guess it was 'Valle's desk' now.

All the old emotions from school blended with how I'd felt when I was last with him. I felt…numb, I guess. A few years ago - heck even a few weeks ago - I would have jumped at the thought of being with Thor, but now, I wasn't sure if I could even work with him.

I glared through his office window at him; he had his feet on the desk. It would probably be no different than working with Hansen, I decided, as it looked like Thor was as complacent as Hansen. At least Thor shouldn't be bothered if I pretended to look busy or not, so I grabbed my book out of my bag and attempted to read it.

"Larsen," Thor startled me, I almost fell off my chair!

"Yes, *Mr Valle*?" I replied sarcastically.

"How's the case coming along?" he asked me.

"Case, Mr Valle? We only have one case, and that is just waiting for the court case to come through."

"Line, you know what I mean."

"Yes, sir, but now the… company dynamics have shifted. You are now my superior."

"Line, the case?" he pleaded with me, with those gorgeous blue eyes of his.

"I've managed, I think, to find the person that Kari *allegedly* murdered," I explained. "A Freya Bergen."

"WOW, that's brilliant, Line!" Thor was impressed. "How?"

"Kari didn't come up on the police's database as a missing person, but no one except us looked at the surveillance footage. Because I did, I managed to get a closer look at who she came to Melshei Forest with. I sent it to the Sandnes office, and they sent back two possible missing girls."

"I'm amazed, well done, Line. How did you find this… Freya?"

"I searched on social media, checked both names that the police disovered until I found the person most closely resembling the victim," I announced proudly.

"Fantastic!"

I smiled at him. It meant a lot for him to be impressed.

"So, both these girls, or women, were missing, do you think?" he asked.

"It seems that way, yes," I confirmed.

He sat down in the chair he had dragged over to my desk. I stared at him in silence, as he tapped a pen onto his lip, deep in thought.

"Do you think they could have been homeless?" I suggested. "Freya didn't seem to have many friends or family that she could stay with."

"She could have just relocated, or had a social media clear out?" Thor added.

"I suppose it's possible," I replied.

"Ok, try searching, just on a normal internet browser, about this Freya, see if there's any news about her disappearance?" he suggested.

I smiled, "Of course, sir."

I swung round and clicked a new tab, and Thor returned to his new office.

He reappeared occasionally, usually to fill up his coffee cup, and it soon needed to be replenished. I ensured that my belongings were securely locked in my drawers and ventured downstairs to refill the jug with water.

I just couldn't shake from my mind that this Freya was homeless but didn't know why.

"I don't like him," a voice interrupted my train of thought.

"Aggie, you startled me."

"Sorry, deary," Aggie replied. "Sure, this new boss of yours is already better than your last one, but there's just something about him that I don't trust."

"Well, it was him who took me to Melshei Forest the other day…"

"Melshei Forest? Mr Valle?"

"Yes, I guess there was just so much going on that we never got the chance to discuss it."

I proceeded to tell her everything about our road trip. She was shocked.

"How dare he!" she ranted.

"It was because of this trip that I was so poorly. I was mainly wearing office clothes, and wasn't dressed for the wilderness."

The front door bleeped; there was a visitor. Aggie muttered and tutted all the way to the door. I smiled to myself and returned to the office. To my surprise, Thor was sitting at my desk.

"I worked out a way to check people online," he announced, still not moving from my seat. I sat on the other chair, moving it up to get closer to the screen.

"If you get the image, in the case of Freya, you can drag it to the search bar, and it'll tell you where the image came from." He demonstrated. "Look."

I peered over to look at the screen. There was an article in an online local newspaper, the Laagendalsposten from Kongsberg.

LOCAL GIRL CAUGHT STEALING FROM GROCERY SHOP

The image was the same as the one we had, which had been used to report her as missing.

"Do you think this is why she went missing, or do you think this is after she went missing?" I questioned.

"She could have stolen food because she was hungry?" Thor suggested. "Which backs up your thinking, that she's homeless."

"Well, I can't believe that she would have hung around after this event," I replied.

"True…true," Thor mused. "OK, can you keep searching for more info about this event, as well as look into any other sightings of her?"

"Yes," I agreed. 'It would be an absolute pleasure', I thought to myself.

I spent the rest of the day trawling the internet, looking for other sightings of Freya. I was only interrupted by a phone call.

"Hello, Hans-"

"It's me, Line," Aggie announced. "There's a handsome young gentleman waiting for you in reception. He's come to escort you home."

"Erik?" I replied.

"Yes, it is the end of your workday, Line."

I looked up at the clock. I had managed to work constantly, even missing my lunch break.

"Ok, Aggie, I'll be down in a few minutes."

I turned off my computer and let Thor know that I was going home. He was playing solitaire on his computer.

"I'm going now, Thor."

He looked at his watch, "Wow, time flies when you're having fun, eh?"

I nodded, and grabbed my bag. "Bye, see you tomorrow!" I called to him as I left.

As I descended the stairs, a pang of guilt overwhelmed me. Spending just a day with Thor had stopped me thinking about Erik. I was such a bad girlfriend!

"Hello, Miss U," he smiled, his blue eyes glistening.

"Hey!" I replied, hugging him.

"Goodbye, Larsen," Thor announced, passing us in the lobby.

I instinctively pulled away from Erik.

"Who's that?" Erik asked.

"Oh, it's the new boss that Hansen hired," I replied vaguely.

Now I was being evasive. Was it for an easy life, or to protect Erik? How was this protecting Erik? It was simply selfishness on my part!

Despite my guilt, we had a lovely evening together. I tried my hardest not to talk about work; firstly, so that we could just focus on each other, but also so that I didn't have to talk about Thor. It wouldn't stop me thinking about him though. How could someone have such an impact on me? And why was it my old crush, rather than my very current boyfriend? I even feigned tiredness at bedtime, to avoid anything too affectionate.

17 – Cold as Stone

Erik must have sensed something, as he had left before my alarm sounded. There was no note, although I knew that he was working the early shift at work.

I intended to make amends; Thor was no good for me, and he was married! Erik didn't need all this, I would focus on him more. I composed a text.

'Good morning, Erik. You left so early, I missed you. Sorry if I was a bit off yesterday, work had been a bit stressful, but I didn't want to burden you with it. Have a good day at work. Come round after and I'll make it up to you?'

I got dressed, in conservative clothes, and left for work. I arrived at the building early, which was intentional – I wanted to try and spend some time with Aggie. She was busying herself around the lobby, as always.

"You missed a bit!" I called to her.

"I can't get it any cleaner, Line!" she rhymed back at me. We both laughed.

"When do you get your cast off?" I asked her, nodding to her arm.

"Not soon enough!" she replied. "It gets itchy quite a lot, so I have to carry a knitting needle around with me."

I frowned, so she demonstrated how she would shove the needle up the cast to scratch parts of her arm where her fingers wouldn't reach. I laughed.

"Your boss is here early," she announced. "I don't like him, Line. He has liar's eyes!"

"Liar's eyes?" I repeated.

"Yes, men like that…" she stopped talking.

I turned around and found that Thor had been behind me.

"Come on, Larsen, time for work."

Aggie looked at her phone and frowned. She knew better than to question other people's business though.

I followed him upstairs.

"We're going on a road trip!" he announced.

"Another one?" I questioned, my heart sinking.

"Yes, but this one is better. We're flying to Stavanger," he explained.

"Wh-Why?" I questioned; I really didn't want a repeat of Sandnes.

"I'll explain on the way. Go grab your notes to take with you, we can brainstorm along the way."

The flight lasted almost three hours, and during that time, Thor told me that Stavanger had one of the highest rates of homeless people in the whole country.

"It's not too far from Kongsberg either," he explained.

I wasn't quite understanding the connection but gave him the benefit of the doubt.

As soon as we were out of the airport, Thor hired a taxi to take us to the centre. It was a beautiful place, not dissimilar to home, except a lot smaller, with quaint little wooden houses and cobble-stoned paths. It brought back all those moments when I'd bump into Thor around our little town, and how the butterflies in my tummy were fluttering. Surely there wouldn't be a homelessness problem in such a beautiful place.

We stopped at a lovely little restaurant for some lunch. Thor called this a brainstorming session.

"I didn't see any signs of anyone homeless, are you sure this is the right place to be?" I enquired.

"They won't just be out on display, would they, Line? That's not good for tourism!"

The only time I'd seen signs of homeless people was on my journeys home from the girls' nights out, passing by a dark corner or asking for spare change outside a shop. That was the darker side of Oslo that I preferred not to think about. I'd led such a sheltered life in our home town, in a place just like this, on the outside. It made me feel unsure about everything.

"We need to look in places where the tourists don't go," Thor said, breaking my thoughts.

"How will we know them, if we don't know our way around either?" I replied.

He shrugged. He didn't have a clue either! He'd insisted that I go on this trip with him, leading me to unknown, potentially dangerous territory. And here we were, divulging in a delicious, expensive meal prior to search for those less fortunate than ourselves.

As we left the restaurant, we ventured through Gamle Stavanger, which was so beautiful. Thor spotted a man, lurking in the shadows of an adjacent building. He approached him, I followed cautiously.

"We're looking for a young girl, old man. Tell us if you know her."

The man shook his head dismissively.

Thor moved along a little further. I stayed where I was, as I was nervous about the potential hostility that I could sense. The last one he approached said he did know who she was, but demanded money to tell him more. Thor backed away from him and we returned to the main streets.

We reached Fisketorget, the local fish market. There was a chill in the air, as expected at this time of the year. I worried for the homeless; how would they, or indeed could they cope with such cold weather? I stopped at one of the stalls that was selling fish soup. I asked for a special order of small cups of the soup, rather than a larger container their customers usually asked for.

As we continued, we stumbled across secluded alleyways where we found the occasional unfortunate. I placed the soups on a bench as I retrieved the pictures of Freya out of my bag. As much as I wanted to help these people, I ensured that my bag was closed and safely tucked away. I felt guilty about assuming they would steal, but survival instincts kicked in.

I crouched down next to a man, wrapped in a blanket as well as having a sleeping bag. He was unshaven, obviously, and looked deep into my eyes.

"I'm so sorry that I am unable to help you," I started. "I don't have a lot of money, but have brought you some soup to warm you up." I passed him one of the cups. "I'm sorry." I showed him the picture of Freya. "My name is Line, and I am looking for this girl? She went missing a few months ago. I'm trying to find her."

"Was she your friend, Line?" the stranger asked.

"No, but I'm extremely worried about her. She isn't as strong as you clearly are, and am sure that she won't be able to cope with the cold as well as you must."

"I don't do it by choice, young lady. I thank you for the soup, but I don't know the young lady."

"Thank you, sir," I replied.

I stood back up and moved along to the next corner, where I spotted someone younger. I repeated my request for information. All the recipients were happy with their soups, although I would have loved to have been able to offer them more.

We turned a corner, and I spotted a woman. I was on the last of my cups of soups, so I'd better make this one count.

"Yes, I know this girl," she replied. "It's Freya, isn't it?"

"Yes, I think that's her name," I replied vaguely, not wanting to 'lead the witness', as they say on tv!

"She used to sit over there," she gestured to another alley. "She always hung around with another girl." She grabbed the other picture I was carrying, the one from the surveillance footage. "Yes, that's her with Freya. I think her name was Jessica? I never spoke to her, but they were always huddled up together. They both left a few months ago."

I almost gasped. "Did they come here together, though?"

"No. Freya had been here for many months. Jessica arrived around Påske."

"Do you know where they went to?" I probed.

She shook her head. "They kept to themselves. It's best to stay in small groups." She showed me a large scar on her arm. "You don't run around on your own when there's people out here that can do this to you. I learned the hard way.

"There was a new man that came into their lives. Freya was in love, and Jessica didn't fit into their plans. Jessica stormed off one day, and Freya tried to keep up with her to reconcile. I never saw either of them again.

"Thank you so much," I touched her hands, and they were so cold. I gave her my gloves. "I'm sorry I can't give you more."

I stood up and started to walk back to the main town. Thor followed me.

"That's it now, can we go? I have all the info we are going to get."

I carried on walking until I found the taxi rank.

"Are you not wanting to make a day of it?" Thor asked, once he caught up with me.

"How can we 'make a day of it' when there are so many… so many homeless people around? I can't offer them money or food, or a roof over their head, so I certainly can't justify sightseeing." I turned to look at him. "If you want to stay, then stay. But I want to go."

"Of course we can go now," he conceded.

Once we reached the airport, we sat down at a coffee shop and had hot drinks.

"It was just so cold," I explained. "And we were only there for a few short hours. These people suffer temperatures worse than that on a daily basis. They have to stay in groups for fear that they will get hurt. That last woman I spoke to, she had a scar on her arm that ran from her wrist to her elbow."

Thor shrugged. "If they choose to live this way of life, then that is up to them. They take their chances."

I looked at him, dumbfounded. "They didn't choose this. They didn't one day decide to leave their old lives behind and live in the worst states imaginable!" I ranted at him.

People started looking at us and staring.

"Look," he started, pulling me close so I could hear his quieter voice, "most of these people aren't as unfortunate as you think they are. They make a career out of this, as it's easier to sit out there all day and collect our money, then they go home. Others do it for drugs, while their government cheques don't pay enough for extras like that."

I gave myself a time out from him, and walked to the toilets to splash some water on my face. My hands were cold since I gave the last woman my gloves, but I found some comfort from the air hand dryer. At least I had that option; those poor people on the streets didn't.

The flight was announced as boarding, so I looked for Thor. He was in the queue to board, not even waiting for me. He had both tickets, so I had to swallow my pride and join him. We sat in silence for the whole flight, which was fine as far as I was concerned.

We landed later than I was due to finish work, and it was only at this point that I checked my phone. I felt the anger build up again, but this time I was angry at me, not Thor. I was neglecting Erik, a lovely man who clearly adored me, simply because of a school crush. Well, to be brutally honest, it was a lot to do with Kari, and finding out who she and Freya were.

I had four missed calls from Erik. I got caught up getting through all the passenger checks, but was finally in a taxi by around six that evening. The taxi driver and Thor were chatting noisily about directions, so making a call was near impossible.

Thor managed to get the driver to drop me off at home. I was hoping that Erik would be there waiting for me, but he wasn't. I called his number, but there was no reply. I left a message, almost grovelling for his forgiveness.

I sat, alone in my little sitting room, drinking a leftover beer from the weekend. I played some music, as I knew I wouldn't be able to focus on tv or a movie; too much was going through my mind.

I pulled my notebook from my bag, and wrote some notes about the day's events. Both girls were homeless, with a very close friendship, although not for more than a few months. The times and circumstances that the last woman shared with me matched the timeline of the incident and that they left together. So what had happened to make one of the girls 'allegedly' murder the other? I needed to see her. I needed to be able to speak to her. She clearly could speak, as there was a witness who saw her talking to Freya, so why wouldn't she speak to those trying to help her? I wrote in my notebook that I needed to make an appointment to see her.

Time was running out. Kari's, well, Jessica's court case date was imminent, as was Christmas. My family were fond of a good get-together at Christmas time, and I had booked the time off work. I was finishing work this Friday. That gave me 2-3 days to get to see her. I'd need money too, to get there and back.

18 – There's a Reason for It

"We need to see her," I announced.

"OK, what's your thinking around this?" Thor questioned me.

I explained all of my thoughts from last night.

He nodded. "OK, I'll check with the prison to see when we can get booked in."

By the end of the day, Thor had gained permission to visit the next morning.

"Book us both seats for the first coach to Halden for the morning, Line, we need to be there by 10:00 tomorrow."

I nodded. "How will we pay for them?" I replied. I knew that I wouldn't be getting my wages until Friday, and wasn't sure what Thor's wages would be.

"Yes, right..." he disappeared into the other office, returning with a credit card.

"This is in Hansen's name?" I questioned.

"Yes, it's the company card that he's asked me to use for anything necessary."

I booked two seats on the first coach out of Oslo and printed off all the necessary documents.

***

The next day I was up early, to ensure that I made it to the coach station on time. I was so excited, hopeful that we could finally get answers to close this case, one way or another. I ensured that I had all the relevant documents with me, including the official paperwork we had received since Kari had become a Hansen and

Associates' client.

I arrived early, but I had skidded a bit on some icy patches on the way. Thor wasn't there yet. In fact, he didn't arrive until just before the coach was ready to leave. I'd had to stand to the side and wait for him, as he had kept the tickets.

The coach was extremely crammed, and it was quite warm as a result, so I removed my outer layers. The seats between myself and my companion were very close together, and I could barely move. I was still a little angry with Thor, but it was difficult to maintain a distance.

"So, what's the plan, Line?! he asked.

"Huh?" I replied.

"Do you have a list of questions for her?"

"She's never spoken to us, so I thought we'd start with the photos we have of Freya, see what happens from there on."

"Seems like a good plan," he commended me, then we were back to silence again.

We arrived at the prison just before 10:00, and had all of our belongings checked by security. We were shown to a room, and then Kari entered.

She looked small, not physically so much, more like…withdrawn, I guess. I wasn't surprised, how would I be in that situation? She sat down opposite us, and I spoke first.

"Hello," I spoke slowly, just in case she was deaf, maybe and I pointed to myself. "Line, Lee-ner," I sounded it out, then I pointed to Thor, "Thorfinn."

I pointed to her. "Jessica?" There was no response.

I pulled out the photos that we had of Freya. "Freya?" I said, pointing at the grainy image from the surveillance photo.

She continued to stare blankly into the small space around us.

I tapped her on the arm gently, to regain her focus. I shrugged. It was an overexaggerated shrug to see if she would understand that we needed answers. Still nothing. This continued for most of the time slot we had been allocated.

"Maybe we should get some drinks?" Thor suggested.

Always thinking of himself, I thought to myself.

"I'm sure that Kari, sorry, Jessica, could do with a decent drink?" I nodded and looked back at the young woman. Thor continued speaking. "En kopp te, frue?"

Kari's eyes flicked from me to Thor.

"Say it again, Thor, but just to her?"

He looked at Kari, held up his pinky finger with mockery. "En kopp te, frue?"

She had definitely understood that. She understood English?

"Quick, do you know any other English?" I frantically asked him.

"Erm… I don't know," he stammered, "Engelsk?"

She sat up and looked at him, just as the guard called that our time is over. I didn't want to leave. I needed to speak to her.

"Do you have a translator here? An English one?" I shouted at the guard. "Engelsk? Engelsk?"

The guard closed the door on Kari, and I strained to look at her through the wired window. She was being escorted away. I was in tears by the time we left the building.

The journey back to Oslo was equally as stuffy as the early one. It was filled to the brim with sweaty bodies. I stared out of the window, trying to stop the tears. I felt a hand hold mine; it was Thor's. I turned to face him and pressed my face against his chest and sobbed as quietly as I could.

"We need to do something, we need a translator," I cried, as we walked up to our office building.

"As soon as I get back in the office, I will contact the prison to book another meeting, and request a translator at the same time. You go home now, you must need the rest after all this."

"O…Ok, thanks," I replied, embracing him again.

I pulled away from him, but he pulled me close and kissed me hard on the lips. "I've wanted to do that for so long," he admitted, wiping away a tear and looking deep into my eyes.

"Line?" a voice behind me spoke. I swung round; it was Erik.

19 – I've Been Losing You

"Erik!" I called, as he turned on his heel and walked away. "Let me explain."

He carried on walking and boarded a bus, just as it was leaving the stop. I stood in silence as I saw the bus leave.

I frantically pulled my phone from my bag and called him; there was no answer. My heart dropped. There was no recovering from this. My head dropped and I walked home sullenly.

I flung my coat and bag on the sofa and sat and cried for a while. Eventually, I pulled myself together enough to check the history on my phone, as I couldn't see any missed calls or texts. The history showed three phone calls from Erik, and a text that read:

'Miss U, Miss U. I'll meet you outside your office after work, and we can have a cosy night in'.

I cried some more, and fell asleep where I was sitting.

***

The rest of the week trudged by slowly. Thor managed to arrange a meeting with Kari, which included an English translator, for the new year, which was just as well, as the court date appointment also came through, for just a week later.

20 – Living a Boy's Adventure Tale

Originally, I intended to go to my parents' home on the Monday, but as I had nothing to stay in Oslo for anymore, I left on the Saturday morning instead. I had tried to call Erik numerous times, but was forwarded straight to voicemail. I sent texts to him, probably at a stalker level, but no response.

Lillianne was my rock, always had been. As teenagers, I had confided in her about everything, so she knew how I felt about Thorfinn. I was a geeky-looking teen, so understood how he would have no interest in me. He had an array of girlfriends at school and was well-admired by all the students. I had been so sure of his disinterest in me that I didn't even tell him. Lilli had suggested that I just get it out in the open, but my best friend had decided that she would give it a go, and she became one of the many.

"Do you not think that it could be 'once a player, always a player'?" she suggested.

"Most definitely," I replied. "Whereas Erik was just perfect."

"I don't think he's an option for you, Line, otherwise he would have answered your calls by now. I think that ship has sailed now."

I sat and sobbed again.

"How can he make me feel so awful and also so…?"

"Happy? No. Content? No. What do you feel for him? Gratefulness?"

"This really isn't helping me much, Lilli," I replied, looking at her through blurred eyes.

"I know what will cheer you up! I don't think it will give you more clarity, but it will make you feel a little better," Lilli announced, jumping up and dashing to her room.

She returned with a hairbrush. I smiled. We spent many a winter's night brushing each other's hair. She sat on the floor on a large, comfortable pillow and stretched out her legs. I sat between them and let the magic happen. The fire was roaring away next to us and the smell of firewood was equally as soothing. It reminded me of childhood, when we would do the ritual hair brushing, but also where we would sit and open Christmas presents or watch tv.

The fire cracked and a burst of orange fire danced up into the air, towards the chimney. I jumped and gasped. That noise, the cracking brought back horrendous memories of Melshei Forest.

Lillianne grabbed me instinctively and held me tight. "Are you ok, Line?"

"Yeah, sorry, the noise, it was just…just, it reminded me of something that happened a few weeks ago that scared me."

"Tell me?"

At that point, Mamma burst into the room. "Girls, can I have some assistance with the feast?"

We both nodded and stood up, with me tying my hair back instinctively.

It sure was a feast. It amazed me every year, and I was amazed how I could forget how magnificent it was to eat too. The table was strewn with edible delights, and we all tucked in. Later, we all sat around the Christmas tree to open presents. It was much more of an adult affair these days, with the alcohol flowing and my body feeling the warmth from both drinks and the fire. I tried to pace myself, I didn't want to embarrass myself, despite how badly I wanted to drown my sorrows. That would have to wait until I got home, I decided, looking at the massive bottle of cider that my parents had given to me as a gift.

For a brief moment, I reconsidered my life options. I was currently living in Oslo, in a lovely little apartment, but that was about all that was working out right for me. My job was going down the pan. I greatly disliked, almost hated, my boss, and the job, with the exception of Kari's case, wasn't all that I had hoped it would be. Maybe the nurturing home environment, with its crackly fire and my family would be an option instead.

Home, where I had the warm fuzzy feelings like this. Why did I leave? Overwhelmed with my momma's pushing to do better. She was of the opinion that my job wasn't high calibre enough for one of her children. What job, career, could I find in Bergen? What about my friends in Oslo? Sure, Erik appeared to be out of the picture now, but I still had Marit, Aggie and the girls.

***

This holiday seemed to be what I needed. There was no rush to my job, or boredom from the lack of work. Mamma wasn't keen on the oversleeping though. Pappa was keen to let me rest and did his best to dissuade Mamma from waking me early, but being the type of person who never relaxes, she was keen to have us out and about. She had planned skiing and hiking for the days between Christmas and New Year.

I figured that the crisp, clean air would blow away my worries, and it did. I'd done very little exercise since I had moved to Oslo, and my body reminded me of this, as my muscles ached intensely. Maybe returning home, to live here or in Bergen would be a good move.

I decided to tell Pappa how I felt, when we had a moment alone. He was busy cooking, as he always seemed to when I was a child.

"I would love nothing more than to have my girls living at home with me," he confided. "Mamma is the complete opposite, of course. There isn't a year that goes by that she doesn't suggest we sell up and move on."

"Your life is here, Pappa," I replied.

I looked intently at my pappa. He seemed happy with life how it was right now, but then he always did. His hair had whitened at a steady rate over the last few years, and he needed glasses, but both just made him look distinguished. He looked smaller to me than I remembered, but really it was my growing taller that had changed.

"And yours will be in Oslo soon enough. Sure, you've hit a slight obstacle right now, but that's just temporary. Work will get better but even if it doesn't, there's more opportunities out there than there are here."

"I just don't know if a law career is right for me."

"It's just a blip. It's your first case, isn't it?" Lillianne had entered the kitchen. "Sorry, I didn't mean to eavesdrop."

"No, not at all," I smiled at her, "more voices of reason are always welcome."

"Things will always work out for the best, I find," Lillianne comforted me. She changed the subject. "Mamma has plans for us tonight, a party at the Solbergs!" Lilli grinned.

We loved to party at the Solberg house. They held one each year, and it was fantastic. Music and drink were mandatory, but they had purchased a hot tub a couple of years ago and that was a bonus. We missed out on it last year, the party and the tub, due to Covid. Mamma has tried to convince them that, in her expert opinion, we would be fine mingling, but the Solbergs were insistent.

We both dashed upstairs to get our swimming costumes and robes, and then spent the next couple of hours getting ready.

"I believe I owe you a hair brushing?" I said, approaching Lilli with the brush.

She sat on the bed with me, and I brushed away.

Once I had finished, I styled it ready for the party.

"Your turn," Lilli said.

"No, it's fine…"

"Well you're not going to the Solbergs with your hair like that," she laughed.

We switched positions, and she started massaging my scalp. "I learned how to do this a few weeks ago, apparently it's good for stress relief, as well as hair growth," she explained. I wasn't complaining, it was divine. "Maybe we can brainstorm tomorrow?"

"Mmmm," I replied.

"I didn't think it would relax you this much," she laughed as she tapped me on the head with the brush.

"Did I nod off?" I asked.

"I didn't think it was possible to fall asleep while sitting up, but clearly you can!"

"I'm sorry," I apologised.

"Don't be, you must have needed it. Now, go get ready, we'll be leaving soon!"

The Solbergs lived about five minutes' walk away, and no one had any intention of driving so we braced the cold night air, as we always had. As we entered, the familiar smell of cinnamon and berries teased our nostrils, and we were confronted by the largest punch bowl I had ever seen. I'd completely forgotten about their legendary punch. I decided to dilute it with some soda water at first, otherwise it would be a very short night for me. Sure, I'd already had a nap followed by a brisk winter walk, but alcohol wasn't generally my friend.

"Ladies," Runa Solberg addressed us, "we will have a schedule for the hot tub tonight. There is a maximum time to be immersed, which is 20 minutes. We have decided to let the young ones in first, so that you can get as drunk as you like after without concern of drowning!"

She laughed like a Disney stepmother but without the malice. Runa was always impeccably dressed. She had the top of the fashion snowsuit every year. For day wear it was always dresses, and for evenings/nights it was usually glitzy and glamorous. This year she didn't disappoint, in an astounding glittery jumpsuit that sparkled as she moved. She was extremely tall, and the jumpsuit embraced that while still accentuating her immaculate figure. She composed herself as if she was the queen, in fact maybe the queen wanted to be awesome as Runa Solberg!

She gestured for us to follow her until we reached the tub. It was already bubbling, so inviting.

"Here is where you can get changed," she opened a door to reveal a room within their cabin, where the tub was housed.

The water was divine, the perfect temperature. The tub had a shelf around the outside where people could place drinks, so I didn't need to worry about splashing water into it – knowing how clumsy I could be.

Lilli joined me moments later and appreciated the water as much as I did. She leant her head back against the rim of the tub and closed her eyes, sighing deeply. I carefully reached for my drink, draining the contents and followed Lilli's lead. I could feel the bubbles tickling me all over. I felt someone brush against my leg. I instinctively moved over slightly to make room.

"It's a good job you aren't brushing my hair in here, Lilli," I laughed. "I'd drown in seconds."

She laughed in agreeance. "Come back to Bergen, and we can share a house that has a hot tub!"

"Don't even joke about it, you know how much I'm struggling about that decision!"

"You're moving back to Bergen?" a new voice broke through my relaxation.

My eyes shot open. "Thorfinn!"

"Why would you move back here? I thought you loved Oslo?" His barrage of questions made me feel dizzy.

I realised it was him touching me. I wanted to get out, but my suit didn't cover much of me, so I stayed in the tub a little longer.

"Time's up, children. Time to get out."

I glanced at Lilli, who instinctively grabbed her robe, which was nearer than mine, and passed it to me to protect my modesty. She stood up and protectively formed a barrier between myself and Thor. He took the hint and exited.

"I'll try and get another chance with the grownups!"

I stood up and wrapped the robe around me. The room in the cabin was heated, so I didn't need to be cold any longer than necessary. I could hear the tub filter self-cleaning. I knew I didn't have long before the next group would be in here, so I dressed swiftly and walked back into the main house. I couldn't see Thor anywhere, so I breathed a sigh of relief.

I still felt a little lightheaded, so I grabbed a soft drink from the fridge. I poured it into a 'posh glass' as we both used to call it when we were children. The adults used to pour lemonade and apple juice into them, pretending that it was champagne or wine. I smiled to myself as I thought of those innocent times. Life was so simple then, even though it didn't seem like it at the time. Homework being late or difficult was as harrowing as it got. Many hours of being consoled by my sister for not understanding the English lessons that we had. My brain just didn't compute languages, whereas Lillianne had made a career out of it.

I wandered around the dining room. It was an incredibly overwhelming room, with a massive wooden table and eight chairs. They had a large cupboard that stretched across the whole of the back wall which used to contain dozens of soda cans, bottles of beers, and savoury snacks all year round, when their children were young. I turned to leave the room to find Thor enter it.

"Hi, Line," he spoke gently, "I'm sorry, I didn't mean to startle you, just now or in the tub." I nodded in acceptance. "Why would you want to move back to Bergen?"

"Things aren't working out the way I hoped they would," I explained.

"I thought things were perfect, personally. We are working together, and I'd hoped that would have been an improvement after Hansen?"

I smiled. "Yes, most certainly. But… but the job isn't as expected. My boyfriend hates me…"

"I don't hate you though."

"You are the reason why my boyfriend hates me," I responded.

"Maybe he's not the one, then?"

I stared at him for a few minutes, trying to figure him out. I couldn't tell if he was toying with me or being serious. His face seemed relaxed, and I couldn't observe any sarcasm in his face or voice. He walked closer to me, sliding his arm around my waist and kissed me, over and over.

"Is this how your boyfriend makes you feel?" he asked me as he pulled away from me.

I shook my head.

"Everything ok in here?" Lilli entered the room.

"Everything is great, thanks Lillianne. Would you two ladies like a drink?"

"That would be great, thank you, Thorfinn," my sister responded.

Once he had left the room, she checked if I was ok.

"It's ok, he just kissed me – again!"

"And how does that make you feel?" she enquired.

"Squiggly!"

"Is that even a word?" she laughed.

21 – Cannot Hide

The next day, I had a wander around town to see if there were any available jobs, and checked out the real estates for places to live.

"The figures just don't match up to my needs," I explained to Lilli when I returned. "The jobs market is rubbish, as I kinda expected, and the housing is so much more expensive than I could afford, if I had to take up a different job, say, like a shop cashier or something."

"So, you stay in Oslo maybe and then keep looking out for stuff, just in case something goes wrong with life over there? There's no rush, is there? You wanted to see this whole case finished, didn't you?" I nodded. "Have you brought your work with you?"

"You know I have because you know what I'm like," I laughed.

"Go fetch it then?" she suggested, and I was in my room and back in a flash. "Ok, so tell me about the basics of it."

"Young female found at Melshei Forest, and picked up by police after a witness called them saying that they thought they had seen her murder someone."

"Ok," she responded, writing it down on fresh paper.

"You're writing it out separately?" I questioned.

"Yes, sometimes people can be too close to something, so a fresh pair of eyes and ears can work a treat," my clever sister explained.

"Ok, the alleged suspect was picked up by police and put into cells. My boss, Mr Hansen went to see her, but she wouldn't talk to anyone."

"Suspect not speaking," Lilli said out loud, as she wrote it down.

"I asked for the report showing what searching the police had done, which they sent to me, but they hadn't found any sign of a victim or other evidence."

"No... victim...," Lilli murmured. "So, they did a full search of the whole forest, but there was no victim?" she questioned.

"Correct," a voice confirmed behind us.

"Thor!" I exclaimed, "...and Kristian." I tried to hide my distaste for Thor's younger brother, but he always seemed to get my hackles up!

"Correct again!" the elder brother smiled.

I tried to compose myself again, as Kris wandered off into the kitchen. "That's all we have, really," I concluded, feeling very flustered.

"Ok, so first things first. Have you got anything about the witnesses?"

"They didn't leave a name but there was a recording that the police sent to me."

"Have you got it here?" Lilli requested.

"Yes, it's on my phone as an mp3."

I dug my phone out of my pocket and found the file.

"Hello? Please help. I've just seen somebody come out of the forest with blood all over her. I think she has killed someone."

"Ok, Miss, stay calm. What is your name? Do you feel like you are in danger too?"

"No, I don't want to give my name. Come quick."

"Ok, where is the exact location please?"

....

"Hello. Are you still there?"

"Play it again?" Lilli requested.

I replayed it.

"Stop there," she asked, when the recording had some white noise. "Just rewind to the static?"

I did as she requested.

"Vi vil ikke at de skal komme for raskt!"

"Huh?" I questioned.

"During the static, some is saying 'Vi vil ikke at de skal komme for raskt' in the background. It's English for 'we do not want them to come too soon'."

Thor and I exchanged glances at the same time. "Kari!"

"Could it be?" I questioned.

"Who is Kari?" Lilli asked.

"She's the suspect. She was named as a Kari Nordmann as she wouldn't tell us her name."

"That doesn't make sense though? Why would she be near enough to be heard over the phone?" Thor questioned.

"Who would be calling the police then? Do you think she was holding the witness hostage?" I asked.

"Not sure about hostage, but maybe forcing her to make the call? It still doesn't make sense though?" Lillianne said.

"What if the victim was the caller?" Lilli threw into the mix.

I shook my head, confused. "It sure as hell doesn't make sense! I think we need to get the surveillance footage at the time of the call. See if they have a camera facing the telephone box. Then maybe we can trace the caller?"

"Agreed," Thor nodded.

"Ok, so there's something new for you," Lilli agreed. "So, you said that the police searched the forest but didn't find anything."

"Yes, that's right. I believe..." I rummaged through my paperwork, "yes, they stopped the search without finding anything, so they must have checked it all? I'd initially thought that Kari could have been the victim, hurt rather than murdered, but there were no injuries on her when we saw her the other day."

"But that was weeks after," Thor mentioned.

"Yes, but I didn't notice anything the first time either. I guess the injuries could have been hidden under her clothes, I suppose. Hansen may have seen something when he visited right at the beginning. Then again, he wouldn't have cared anyway, as long as he gets his fee at the end of the trial!"

Lilli looked through her notes. "How can they arrest someone for murder if there is no evidence and no victim? And I assume that they can't find the 'witness'?"

I shrugged. Kristian walked into the room and snatched some of my notes out of my hands. With a mouthful of food, he started reading portions of my notes out loud. I looked at Thor for help, but he just laughed. That was something from school that I definitely didn't miss.

"Are you all going to the New Year party at Catrine Bystrom's house tonight?" Kris asked.

"Depends, are you going?" I replied sarcastically, despite it being near truth!

"Wouldn't miss it for the world!" he announced, throwing my papers all around the room. "I'm in there, with that Catrine!"

We all burst out laughing and he threw the rest of the fruit tart that he was eating at me. I breathed deeply for a few minutes, to keep me calm. Lilli disappeared to find something to clean us with, and gathered up the papers.

"I'm definitely going too," Thor leaned over to me and whispered, "I think I'm in there with that Line girl!"

I felt my whole body quiver, and my mouth went dry.

"I thought you said he was married, Line?" my sister questioned as we were getting ready for the Bystrom's party.

The Bystroms were even more famous for their parties than the Solbergs were. Anybody who was anybody would celebrate New Year with them, in their glamourous house. For me personally, I'd much rather be in the Solberg's tub than watching their fireworks. Maybe the Bystroms should upgrade and do both! They were at the Solberg's party the other night, so were probably already shopping around for a bigger and better tub. Next year would bring us the answers!

"Huh?" I replied.

"Thor, you said he went to Oslo to get married?"

I had completely forgotten about that. "I'll ask him in a few days, when all the festivities are over. Surely she would be here if there was a Mrs Valle?"

Lilli shrugged and zipped her dress up. My sister was so beautiful, so lucky. Anything she wore was enhanced by her natural beauty, and this red, figure-hugging dress that sat way above the knee was spot on. Me, on the other hand, was last in line when it came to beauty or brains; I had neither.

"You look beautiful," a voice behind me seemed to have read my mind; I was sure that I hadn't said it out loud.

"Hardly," I snorted, and turned round to see Pappa.

"All of my girls are equally beautiful!!" he argued.

I raised my eyebrows. He always made the effort to make me feel as special as Lilli.

Mamma didn't have the same courtesy. "I think the black dress would have looked better on you, Line," she said to me just a moment after Pappa's compliment.

"No, I think the blue is perfect for her!" Pappa defended me. "Brings out the colour in her eyes."

I smiled. "Thanks, Pappa, you always have my back."

We had arranged for a cab to take us to the Bystroms as they lived much further away from us than the Solsbergs. If I knew how to drive, I would have happily driven and not drank. Maybe that could be my New Year's resolution for next year?

As the cab approached the Bystrom's house, I gasped. Every year they seemed to have more lights than before, and this time they had deer wire statues adorned with beautiful white lights. This is what I hoped for when I had a husband and children.

"You look stunning," Thor declared when he saw me. I wasn't convinced, but smiled at him anyway. "You know what would make it look even better?" I braced myself for the 'on the bedroom floor' joke that was imminent.

Instead, he pulled out a little velvet pouch from his pocket. I frowned. He passed it to me.

"Open it then."

I did just that, and revealed a beautiful, sparkly bracelet. I gasped, it was gorgeous.

"But…I didn't get y-"

"Shush, I insist. Let me help you put it on." He carefully draped it over my wrist and clipped the clasp together. "There!" he said, brushing his hand along my inner arm, making the tiny hairs stand up on end at his touch.

It was almost electrifying. I held my breath. He ran his hand from my wrist, up my arm, then neck and then the back of my head. He looked deep into my eyes and moved his hand round to brush my cheek.

"Yo, bro, you gotta come and see this!" Kristian announced excitedly, grabbing his brother by his arm and dragging him away.

I remained exactly where he left me until Lilli found me a while later. She had found me mesmerised by my new gift.

"Ooh that's very sparkly."

I nodded, still speechless. She thrust a drink into my hand, and I downed it in one go, not even knowing what it was.

"That bad?" she enquired.

"Thor gave it to me," I explained.

"I gathered that," she laughed. "It is beautiful."

"Do you think he actually bought this, for me?"

"Why not…?"

"Because he's never really shown any interest in me before the last few weeks."

"He works with you now, yes?" she asked.

"Yes…?"

"And you have had a payday just before you came here?"

"Yes…"

"And he kissed you before you both left Oslo?"

"Yes…"

"So he could have trawled around the shops before he left Oslo?"

"Yes… but surely he would have given it to me before today?"

"Who knows how a man's brain works," Lilli laughed.

Catrine joined us for some small talk. She was the daughter of single mamma, Hilde Bystrom, who was hosting this party. Catrine was rather plain looking, with her brown hair tied into a simple ponytail, no makeup and was wearing a plain grey dress.

"Mamma said I neded to mingle," she explained. "It doesn't matter if you don't like me, just pretend for a few minutes and then I'll go again."

She was kind of sombre, and had been all through school, Lilli had told us. Catrine was mid-20s, I believe, so Lillianne had been a few years below her in school.

"It's years since I have seen you, Catrine," I greeted her. "What are you doing with yourself these days?"

She looked at me blankly for a few seconds. "I…I work for the travel agency in Bergen." She looked at Lilli. "The one we used to all steal brochures from and dream of distant shores."

Lilli smiled.

"Oh that's great, Catrine, you are so lucky!"

"It's not been so good through Covid, many of us thought we were losing our jobs."

"That must have been scary," I sympathised. "Are you going on any holidays next year?" I was determined to keep the conversion going, to make her feel included.

She nodded. It was proving difficult, and she started to become reserved again; then I realised that Kristian was hovering around us.

"Could you show me your Christmas decorations in the front garden? They looked great but didn't get the chance to look at them properly."

She looked at me, gauging my intentions. "Sure."

Out in the front garden, which was below zero, I explained that I just wanted to get her alone to see how she felt about Kristian.

"Kristian? The boy who is about ten years younger than me?"

I nodded.

"Nothing but distaste," she admitted.

"Me too," I giggled. "Well, just a head's up, I think you may be the target for a liaison later."

She laughed heartily. "Not a chance!"

I smiled and we went back indoors.

We drank and danced all night. Thor joined in for a little grind – I hoped that the bracelet didn't mean that he was allowed to do anything that he wanted to. Catrine made an extra special effort to avoid Kristian.

Shortly before midnight, we all gathered outside to watch the immense firework display. Afterwards, the crowd started to dissipate and Thor coaxed me into the small utility room for more privacy. There was a moment when he attempted to get more intimate by lifting me up onto the washing machine, but I sobered up rather quickly and calmed the situation down.

My first time with Thor was not going to be amongst the Bystrom's underwear. It was, however, amongst the clean sheets of my bed once the rest of my family had gone out skiing for the day. I wasn't feeling well enough to to ski, but did manage some hygge time with my… boyfriend?

22 – You'll End Up Crying

We both returned back to Oslo separately, as our tickets had been booked on different journeys. I had bid my family farewell, feeling a bit happier about returning; partly because Thor would be there, and partly to solve Kari's case.

I couldn't wait to go back to work on the first Tuesday back in Oslo. I missed Lillianne and Pappa; Mamma, not so much! Now that Thor was my boyfriend and was working with me, I felt a bit happier. I was excited to progress further with Kari's case too, and my first job was to contact the surveillance company for footage of the caller. Our visit with Kari was booked for Thursday, and the court case was to begin on the following Monday. It was tight, but doable.

Thor wasn't concerned about what other work I was doing, and we spent the majority of the time kissing in his office. Well, to be precise, that was only until Aggie called to remind me that the offices had cameras – I'd completely forgotten. Thank goodness we didn't go any further.

"Thor, I keep meaning to ask you – aren't you married?" I'd broached the subject while I was sitting on his lap.

He frowned and looked at me, puzzled.

"You came to Oslo to get married. That's what you told me in the coffee shop when we first met here," I explained.

"Ah, you must mean Jeanette."

"Ok?" I replied, confused.

"I met Jeanette a couple of years ago. She was moving to Oslo for work last summer, for a holiday club for children. I automatically wanted to follow her, I thought it was love that I felt for her. We both moved here, but by the end of the summer, instead of getting married, like we had planned, she got a job working in a school in China. It was just too far for me, and I had just enrolled at college, so she went without me."

"Oh, how sad. Is she coming back?" I questioned.

"I don't know, she just ended all contact with me once she went there."

"And you are ok now?"

He had kissed me. "Very ok!" he replied.

He fetched lunch for us both, and I stayed in the office in case there were any calls.

He soon returned with crab salads for us both. "I figured, if you feel as overfed since Christmas as I do, a nice light salad would be great," he explained when I examined it.

"Sure," I responded, craving chocolate and naughty foods.

It was better than I thought it would be, but I was determined to grab a hot chocolate from Marit's after work. In the meantime, I drank copious amounts of sweet coffee.

Thor decided that we could leave early as there wasn't much work here. We switched off everything in the office and he arranged with Aggie to have the calls diverted to her instead. I tried to stop for a chat with Aggie, but he stood at the door, waiting for me to go with him. I promised that I would speak to her tomorrow, and left the building.

I automatically started walking to the café, but Thor stopped and asked why I was going the wrong way. "Oh, I thought we were clean eating," he announced.

"Yeah, sure, I was just going to see Marit. I've not seen her this year yet."

"Oh, right, let's go then."

We arrived at Marit's and she waved at me. I introduced her to Thor, and she asked me what I wanted to buy. I didn't really want anything … healthy, and Thor stood at my side the whole time, so I explained that I just wanted to say hi and we left.

Thor followed me home. We chatted all night about old times at school, and also about our recent visit back home. With all the happy memories flooding back to me, I felt fuzzy and cosy inside.

23- Start the Simulator

We found that we had overslept the next morning, and had to rush and fight over the bathroom to enable us to both get to work. We arrived about half an hour later, but it had been worth it. We had discussed taking the day off and just staying in bed, but I had too much to sort out in time for my visit with Kari tomorrow.

First on the agenda was to check for the email with the footage attached. There was nothing in my inbox regarding it, so I refreshed the coffee and collected the mail, which would give me the opportunity to catch up with Aggie. She'd had a quiet Christmas with her husband and sons.

"Looks like your Christmas turned out great," Aggie commented.

"Oh, yes," I beamed.

"What about that other young man that you were with? I liked him much better." Aggie didn't beat around the bush; life was too short, apparently.

I gave her the basic run down of events, but was interrupted by a phone call. I stepped back to allow her some discretion.

"It seems as if Mr Bossman was too busy to answer your phone," she divulged after the call ended, pulling a face and passing me a slip of paper.

"I guess I better get back, then! I'm hoping to be able to pop out for a hot chocolate shortly, will see how it goes."

Back in the office, I looked at the note. It was a message from Hansen – that was all I needed! I rang him straight back.

"Hello Mr Hansen, apologies, I had just nipped to the toilet. It's ladies-"

"That's far more information than I needed," he cut me off. 'Ladies problems' was always a sure-fire way to make him flustered. "I was just checking to make sure that everything is running smoothly. I see that the court case date has finally come through."

"Yes, it's Monday."

"Unfortunately I can't make it. I shall get Mr Valle to pay for you both to attend on my behalf."

"Oh ok, Mr Hansen."

"Transfer me through to Mr Valle."

I dutifully did so, and I could see Thor look at the phone and ignore it.

"It's Hansen, Thor, he specifically asked to speak to you," I shouted over to him.

He sat up and answered, motioning to me to shut his office door.

I felt a little awkward watching him on the phone, so made some fresh coffee. I suddenly realised that because Thor was on the phone to Hansen, it meant he couldn't check up on me answering calls, so I sneakily took a short trip to Marit's.

"Hello, Marit, so sorry about yesterday."

"Who was the hunk? What happened to the other guy? I liked him."

I laughed, "Apparently everyone did. I screwed up. Neglected him and treated him really bad. I've been in love with Thor for years now, and he kissed me just before Christmas, and Erik saw us."

"Were you cheating on him then? If it has been going on for years…?"

"No, no it was more a schoolgirl crush, really. That kiss was the first one. It was just unfortunate that he was there. But we used to both live around Bergen, and got together there, over Christmas."

I handed her my cup, changing the subject. "Do you make sugar-free hot chocolate, by any chance?"

She frowned, "Yes, we do. Is that what you want?"

"God no! Thor seems to be on a health kick, so if he is with me and I'm ordering hot chocolate, I may ask for one, but still want that SUGAAAR!" I laughed.

"Did you want me to hide the marshmallows then?" she suggested.

"Won't they still float to the top though? I'll skip the marshmallows, for now!" She nodded and whipped up a drink in no time.

"I should probably get going, before the boss catches me."

By the time I returned, there was an email from JLR Surveillance. I clicked it excitedly and found an mp4 file attached. I opened it up. I made a point of watching it completely so that I didn't miss any important information this time.

The angle of this camera was obviously pointed away from most of the entrance where the two women entered, but I did spot a little of Freya's shoes at they turned. I watched vigilantly. It was a very busy place for visitors, but I stuck with it until 13:08, the time of the call.

I stood up, my chair flying backwards, and rushed into Thor's office. He looked up.

"The caller," I announced, "it's FREYA!"

"Oh my God, no way?!"

"Yes, and Kari is with her. It is definitely her who was speaking English in the background."

I forwarded the email to my own, so I would have a copy of it on my phone for our visit tomorrow.

24 - Lamb to the Slaughter

The information we had received just caused more questions for me, so I started to write a list.

My initial questions had been:

- *Why was she homeless?*
- *Why did they go into the forest?*
- *Had they known each other before they were homeless?*

I couldn't even get the new questions straight in my head right now.

"You've got plenty of time, Line," Thor said, breaking my thoughts.

I turned and smiled at him. "I need to have the questions written down so that I don't miss anything."

"Not right now though. Come to bed, we need to be up early in the morning."

I couldn't sleep, even with Thor having no trouble himself. I occasionally thought of another question, so I wrote it down in the notebook that I had taken to be with me.

Why was it faked? That was my main question.

Why would Kari want to go to prison? It was clear that no one had been killed that day, or even hurt.

Now that we knew that she was English, why was she in Norway? Why couldn't she go back home? That was why she couldn't be found, why she wasn't on the missing person's system – because it was just a Norwegian list. We needed to find a way to obtain the use of the international system to search for her. We wouldn't be able to do it tomorrow morning, before the meeting, but maybe in the afternoon?

Thor woke me up the next day. I wasn't sure when I'd fallen asleep. At least I had a couple of hours on a coach to think of more questions. Thor had already showered and was ready to go. I looked at the time on my phone; I had just enough time for a quick shower. I remembered that last time we were there it had been a bit of a walk after the coach, so made sure that I dressed accordingly. Pappa had bought me a jumper for Christmas. It was off-white and cable knit, and I happily pulled it over my top and could almost smell Christmas on it. I was ready to go, and Thor was relieved.

We had to take a taxi to the coach stop as we'd take too long to walk it. The journey to the prison seemed shorter this time - probably because I wasn't fully ready as I didn't yet have all the questions. My stomach growled. We hadn't had time for breakfast and hadn't packed anything for the journey. At best, we had five hours until I'd be able to get anything to eat. I closed my eyes to try and think of more things that I needed to know.

"So, Hansen was saying that he needs us both to accompany Kari at court on Monday. She needs to plead guilty to murder, as they are saying that she willingly went into the forest with the victim purely to kill her."

"But she didn't?" I interrupted.

"We have no proof of that, and this is what our boss wants." I nodded and put my head down. "If she takes the plea deal that is on offer, she will only be incarcerated for 15 years to life, rather than life without the possibility of parole."

Surely there was something that we could do, to get her to not go to jail. She had already spent the last three months locked up.

As we alighted the coach at Halden's stop, the cold air hit me like a thousand knives to my face. I wrapped my scarf around as much of my face as I could. This was about the coldest I had ever felt. I

thought about all those homeless people in Stavanger, and how difficult it must be for them. We pushed through the biting wind that was pushing against us, to get to the prison in time for our meeting.

We passed what must have been the exercise yard, and there was a thick sheet of white ice there. It must be awful to have to stand out there for the one-hour exercise they were forced to do.

The prison was like a completely different climate, like summer had arrived. I quickly removed all my outdoor clothes along with the jumper my pappa had bought me. We were allowed straight into the room and Kari was already there waiting for us.

"We were expecting an interpreter or translator for the meeting," I asked when two of the guards left us.

The last guard nodded, "She is on her way."

"Will this time cut into our small appointment time?" I replied, getting slightly agitated.

"You are not restricted today, you can stay as long as you wish, within reason, of course. It is your last time with your client until court on Monday."

Without the aid of the translator there was little that we could do. Neither of us could speak English. I'd prepared questions, sure, but I hadn't prepared for not being able to talk to her to ask her the questions.

"Lee-ner," Kari stated.

I swung round. "Yes, that's me," I replied, pointing to my chest.

She smiled. "Jessica," she responded, pointing to her chest.

I cried with joy. I'd always thought it was a cliché, but I was literally overjoyed. I took my phone out of my bag and opened up the mp4. I passed the phone to Jessica, and she clicked to watch it.

"Vi vil ikke at de skal komme for raskt," I said, reading a scrap of paper that my sister had given me.

I was sure it was probably the worst translation in English ever, but she looked at me; she knew what I had meant. I pointed to her and Freya in turn, stating their names and she nodded.

The door creaked and the translator entered.

"Lillianne!" I screeched, most likely too loudly, as the guard reverted to his attack stance. "Wh…What are you doing here?" I asked, standing up and hugging her.

"I'm registered within the prison system as a translator. I've only done it once before, but jumped at the chance when I spotted this job yesterday on their website."

"Hi, Lilli," Thor greeted her.

"Jessica?" she spoke softly.

Jessica nodded.

They then had a long conversation in English, which made absolutely no sense to me.

She held out her hand. "Can I have your notebook full of questions?"

"I didn't get much time to add to the list, unfortunately," I replied, ashamed of my inability.

"It doesn't matter, let's start with what we have."

She turned back to Jessica and continued her conversation. The guard in the room pointed to where there was a small cafeteria and told us we could get some food and drink there while Lilli worked.

"I can't believe that we've acquired the best translator in the world," I exclaimed with pride, while filling my face with a plate of eggs.

When we returned to the meeting room, Lilli smiled at me. "Do you want a tour of the prison, Line? Unfortunately, men aren't allowed in the women's section, though."

"I'd love to," I agreed excitedly, without realising that Thor might not want to be left on his own.

"Excellent, Jessica thought it'd be a good idea."

Keeping it professional, I smiled at Thor and followed the others. We walked for a short time and then we were in a kitchen. It looked quite like mine actually, very small.

"How are the chefs able to use such a small kitchen?" I asked, when I saw how only the three of us really fit in there.

Lilli asked Jessica. "It's just a kitchen for a couple of inmates. They cook their own food."

"Really?" I was astonished. "What about all the sharp knives, and fires, and…"

Lilli nodded.

We left the kitchen and she pointed into another room. I entered first, and it was amazing. There was a wooden-framed bed, a matching desk and wardrobe, a tv, and even an ensuite bathroom.

"It's better than a hotel!" Lillianne said when she followed me in.

Jessica pointed to a box under the tv; it was a games console. She left the room and we followed her around some more. There were different rooms for learning. She pointed to one and said, "Norwegian," smiling proudly.

There was a fantastic sports hall and a recreation room, with pool tables, table tennis, sofas and tv – a social room.

"WOW," I summarised, "it's certainly better than sleeping on the cold streets, isn't it?"

Back in the meeting room, Thor announced that we had to leave very soon or we'd miss our coach, so Jessica said goodbye to us, in Norwegian, and went to get some food. My big sister gave me a huge hug and we went our different ways to get to our homes.

"So, what happened then? Did we get all the answers we needed?" Thor asked during the journey home.

"Most of them," I nodded.

25 – Shadow Endeavors

It was Friday, and I was meeting up with my friends tonight. I spent the morning arranging transport and accommodation for Sunday, as we had to stay closer to the court and Thor had decided that it would be easier if we were there. Hansen had left him in charge, and it was an 'executive decision', Thor claimed.

Thor left at around 11:00 as he had to be at college for the afternoon, so I went back to the chair-swirling again. I still had some unanswered questions which I felt I deserved answers to, seeing how much work I put into the case, so as I thought of questions, I continued to write them down.

I left the office, and nipped to Marit's to get a naughty hot chocolate, grateful to not have to answer to Thor for once. Of course, I had thoroughly enjoyed all the time I had been spending with him, but little things like a girl's night out and a hot chocolate were loved too. I stayed and chatted with Marit for a while – without worries of repercussions – but not for too long as I had to get changed. I skipped out of her shop.

As I turned the corner past the office building, I felt a massive thump to my side, so severe that I smacked my head against a wall. It was well-known that I was clumsy, but I didn't remember slipping. I tried to compose myself, but this time the thump was even harder, and my face was pressed up against the wall.

"Stop sleeping with MY husband," a voice hissed into my ear.

I wasn't sure if it was Heidi, or maybe Thor's almost-wife? I turned around to be face-to-face with Mrs Hansen.

"Mrs Hansen…" I attempted to proclaim my innocence, but a third shove against the wall stopped me in my tracks.

"STOP sleeping with my HUSBAND!" the voice grew louder.

"I'M NOT!" I screeched back at her, an unknown anger rising in me. "Neither is Mrs Johnsen, but I agree on one thing - he's certainly acting cagey." Heidi loosened her grip and stepped back slightly. "Let me help you?" I continued. "I saw him in a coffee shop a few days ago with a mysterious blonde woman. I really felt for you, didn't want to see anyone treat a fellow female hurt like that."

"I don't want pity," she responded, pushing me up against the wall again.

"No, too right you don't!" I felt brave now. "You want answers, you want it to be known that you aren't crazy, like people may think - like your husband thinks."

"Yes. But I love him so much," she stated.

"But do you, though, Mrs Hansen? He's treating you this way. Making you feel all these alien emotions. You shouldn't need to act like that. Let me help you. What I suggest, and it's just a suggestion for you to think about, you stay away from the office, from me and Mrs Johnsen. No threats, no phoning up to see where he is. He won't like it if you aren't this… this passionate about keeping your marriage safe. I shall talk to Mrs Johnsen and her boss, Mr Olsen, about letting K… Mr Hansen back into the office, and that way we can keep an eye on him. Let's see if we can get some evidence of his cheating on you, to put your mind at rest. What do you think?"

"But how do I know it is not you having the affair?"

"You'll have to trust me, but I promise you that I'm not, and neither is Mrs Johnsen. She loves her husband and sons so much. Heidi, can I call you Heidi?" She nodded. "Heidi, I will log times for when he is in or out of the office. We, you and me, can put our notes together to look for gaps in his timeline, times when he's not at home or at work.

"I'll see if I can get photo evidence of anything. We shouldn't be using violence to solve this. We are intelligent women, let's put our heads together and sort it out. Whether you will want him back or not, you will hold the winning hand and it'll be your CHOICE!"

Heidi stepped back and returned her arms to her side. She nodded. "Yes."

"I can't get the restraining order lifted, unfortunately, but you don't need to be anywhere near us. Do you have a mobile number that I can text you on?"

She nodded again, and entered her details into the phone that I had handed her, and I did the same. Our names were listed as LL and HH, our new code names.

"I'm so sorry," she muttered, backing away from me.

As quick as she had arrived, she left again. I slid to the floor and cried.

I shakily took my phone back out of my pocket, wanting to ring Thor to come and get me, but I knew he was busy at college. I wasn't that badly hurt; some grazing on my face and arm maybe. Just superficial wounds, which would be gone in a few days.

I put my phone back in my pocket and tried to stand up, but my foot wouldn't let me put any pressure on it. Knowing that Aggie was still in the building, I hobbled back towards the door. She spotted me and smiled, opening the door for me. As soon as she saw me, she could see that I wasn't my usual, happy self.

She brought me into the reception area and closed the blinds. "What happened, Line?"

I told her all that had happened, including the deal we had made. She was wary at first. I felt like I had gotten through to Heidi but obviously Aggie had also been on the wrong side of Mrs Hansen too. She grabbed her phone to ring for emergency services. I tried to talk her out of it.

"I don't think I'm hurt too much, just a little shaken," I explained.

She took no notice of my pleas, and a paramedic and police officer arrived pretty soon afterwards. They tended to my wounds at the office, and I rang Belle to say that I couldn't make it to dinner tonight. I started crying and told her what had happened.

"Don't move," she insisted. "If Aggie can stay for an extra 15 to 20 minutes, then that'd be great."

I asked her, and she nodded.

Within 10 minutes, Belle and Astrid had arrived, ready to help me to get home. Once back, Belle washed some dirt off my face, and Astrid got some glasses out of my cupboard and produced a bottle of wine out of her bag. She poured me a very large glass full and I drank about half in one go. There was a knock at the door around half an hour later, and I jumped, fearing who it could be. Belle opened the door. It was Helene, with takeaway Chinese food. We tucked in. I so needed this, and it was made even better having my great friends here with me.

"We'll sort out finding a self-defence class. We are strong, powerful women, and need to be able to protect ourselves from others, if necessary," Helene announced.

"Not this weekend, though, I hurt a little," I begged.

"Of course, but soon!"

26 – The Way We Talk

"So what's the issue with Thor then?" Belle asked me the following day, trying to divert my attention away from Heidi.

I had confided in her that I was unsure as he had been crowding me.

"Hmmm, I don't know really, it just seems that he's not willing for me to have too much independence. I'd never had a boyfriend before Erik, so I'm not sure what the standard is. I know that my parents are still together and they have different careers, and both have space from each other."

"You have to do what you feel suits you both. You are allowed to have your own interests and pastimes, and time apart."

"Hmmm," I replied. "I liked how it was with Erik."

"You don't need to be in a relationship that doesn't seem right, especially if you are preferring your ex."

"Thor was the one, you know, I loved him for so many years," I explained.

Belle put her hand on my knee, "I'd hug you, if it didn't hurt you!"

She stood up and wandered into the kitchen to make some hot chocolates for us both. I'd managed to hide some marshmallows at the back of a cupboard.

"There's a classic example," I continued, "He's put us on a health kick, so I'm having to hide my hot chocolate mix and marshmallows. You shouldn't need to hide things like that from a boyfriend, should you?"

"You are allowed your guilty pleasures."

"Yes, but he watches everything I eat, and feeds me salad for every meal, with fruit for breakfast."

"Speak to him," she suggested. "Set things straight before it gets too advanced."

I nodded, "Yes."

There was a knock at the door. Belle walked over to the spyhole.

"It's Thor," she whispered.

I shook my head and put my finger to my lips.

She crept back to where we had been sitting.

"I can't let him in. Not only am I drinking forbidden hot chocolate, but if he sees all my grazes and bruises, he'll never leave my side!" I whispered.

He knocked a couple more times, then it seemed to go quiet again.

"At least we aren't planning to go out today," Belle laughed.

We spent the rest of the weekend binge-watching Disney films and eating naughty snacks, right up until it was time for me to leave for court on Monday.

"Where have you been?" Thor enquired, then his face softened when he saw my injuries. "What the hell happened?"

"I was attacked on Friday on my way home from work."

"Who? Have they caught them?"

"It was Mrs Hansen. She was determined that I was having an affair with Hansen."

He approached me and tenderly touched some of my sore parts.

"Oh, some of the bruises look really sore. And your face? Oh, I'm going to make sure she goes to prison for this!"

"No, it's fine, we got it all sorted already."

He hugged me for what seemed like ages, until it was time for us to leave for our journey.

We travelled in silence for the most part. Thor carried my clothes bag and made sure that life was as easy as possible. I felt a little guilt with this, after all I had told Belle just yesterday.

27 - Celice

The hotel was beautiful. Very high spec, with soft, comfortable beds, a tv and even a minibar. Thor slept well, holding me tightly in his arms for the most part; my sleep was fitful and nightmare-filled. I eventually got up at around 06:00. I took advantage of the bath that was there and soaked to relax myself. At first, the scratches and grazes stung from the hot water, but that wore off quite quickly.

I dressed quietly and sat in the comfy chair, catching up on emails. I re-watched the footage of Jessica and Freya going into Melshei Forest, and Freya making the call to the police. I listened to the recorded emergency call over and over. I read through all of my notes, and copied the notes from our last visit into the notebook I used exclusively for this case. Something just wasn't right.

Where was Freya? I remembered the discussion with the woman on the streets of Stavanger, who knew the two young women. "There was a new man that came into their lives. Freya was in love, and Jessica didn't fit into their plans. Jessica stormed off one day, and Freya tried to keep up with her to reconcile. I never saw either of them again."

Why now? The visit with Jessica was spinning around in my head. Walking into the prison from outside was like a different climate. It was a welcome relief. It was the perfect time to end up in prison really, it was getting cold when we were in Stavanger, but we only had a few hours of that; these people had it for a fair few months of the year.

It all started to make sense…

I heard Thor mumbling as he began to wake up. "Good morning," I whispered, not wanting to startle him.

"Good morning, princess," he replied, stretching.

He climbed out of bed and into the bathroom. I closed my eyes to get the information into some kind of order in my head. He had a shower and then he was ready to go to the restaurant for breakfast.

I suddenly had quite an appetite; my injuries were out of my mind for now, replaced by my newly-found knowledge – I had cracked my first case. I ate more than Thor would have allowed usually, but he just seemed grateful that I was on the mend, mentally at least. I had a couple of plates full, from the all-you-can-eat breakfast buffet, washed down with plenty of coffee

We proceeded to the courthouse once our bellies were full. We were a little early, but it gave us more time to prepare. I was buzzing, and it wasn't just the caffeine! I looked around the waiting area that we had been advised to sit in, and at the entrance, I saw Lillianne. I stood up and hugged her, and she enquired about my wounds. I'd completely forgotten about that.

"Oh, it is nothing to worry about, I will explain later. What are you here for, Lilli?" I asked.

"They needed me to interpret the case, so that Kari, sorry Jessica, understands the repercussions of each plea."

"Great. It's good to see you."

Thor fetched us some drinks from the vending machine. "She's wired from the amount of caffeine she's had," he laughed. "I got you a green tea, Line."

"I have solved the case," I blurted with excitement, once we were all settled.

"Really?" Lilli replied, looking at both Thor and myself.

Thor shrugged. "It's news to me."

"Sorry, Thor, it all came to me while you were asleep and during breakfast."

"Ok, so spill then," my sister said.

"Well, we are definitely doing a plea deal. As much as I want to not send a young woman to prison for 15 plus years, it needs to be done. It's better than being on the streets, especially at this time of year."

"Ok, and...?"

"That's why she's in prison, why they staged the murder. To get Jessica off the streets, and somewhere warm and dry. Three meals a day and a roof over your head. Despite being surrounded by violent inmates, she's safer here than in Stavanger!"

I watched as Thor's face showed the realisation of what I had just said.

"Where's Freya though?" he asked.

"That's the only part she wouldn't tell us. Didn't want to jeopardise the sentence or betray her friend's confidence, I guess?"

"Wow, my mind is blown!"

We were called into the courtroom, and Jessica was walked in with two guards. Thor joined her at the table towards the front, as he was her legal representation in lieu of Hansen not being here. Lilli squeezed my hand, and then joined them both. I sat behind them.

The courtroom started to fill with a few reporters, but not many others as there was no official victim, and Jessica had no family to support her. A young lady in a blue dress sat down next to me, and a man next to her. I raised my head to smile politely.

"Freya," I gasped.

The woman nodded. "I was, once. Obviously, this can't be revealed here, today."

The man leant over her. "Hello, I'm Kol."

"Kol is my husband. We got married last week," Freya announced.

I smiled. "Congratulations. What is your name, madam? I didn't catch it."

"Celice," she replied.

Our attention was directed back to the front of the room.

"Good morning, ladies and gentleman," the judge began. "We are here to discover the sentence of the defendant, in the case of the murder of an unknown person. Can the defendant please tell us her name?"

My sister spoke quietly to Jessica.

"Jessica Jane Smith," Jessica addressed the judge.

"Do you, Jessica Jane Smith understand that you can plead guilty, which means that you carried out a murder on another human being, whether found or unfound, which was premeditated; or not guilty, which means we will involve a lengthy court case with a jury present, which, if found guilty will incur a longer sentence than by taking the plea deal?"

Lillianne repeated this information to Jessica, who in turn said, "Yes."

"And do you, Jessica Jane Smith, plead guilty or not guilty?!

My sister leant over to Jessica and pointed to a sheet of paper which contained the words GUILTY and NOT GUILTY, for her to choose.

"Guilty," Jessica announced.

"Thank you for your plea, Miss Smith. You will be sentenced to serve a minimum of 15 years in Halden Prison. Guards, take her away."

Jessica turned round and smiled at me, and then at Freya and Kol. They both stood and blew kisses to her.

"Jeg vil besøke deg så ofte som mulig," Freya shouted to her.

"Jeg ser frem til det, fru Lindgren," Jessica replied.

I felt quite emotional about the outcome of the case.

I turned to Freya. "What did you just say to each other?"

"Just that I would visit her as much as possible, and that she would look forward to it."

"Did you choose this so that you could get married?" I questioned.

"Partly," she replied. "It was getting cold, I knew Jessica wouldn't be able to cope with the cold. England, although cold, is nowhere near as cold as gets here in Norway. Also, once 2020 hit, the amalgamation of the prison to allow women was a perfect option for her."

There was only one other question remaining, "Why was Jessica in Norway rather than England? "

"She had a bad time with her family, and took solace in music, when she discovered a music band based here in Norway. She found them on the internet, and decided she wanted to find them. It was a poor decision, and she found that she had no money to return, nor an interest in going back, so she settled here, and found me. I now move forward with the knowledge that she will be safe and warm."

I nodded, a tear in my eye. Lillianne and Thor turned to return to me.

"We must be going now, we don't want to stay here any longer than necessary," Kol commented.

"I understand," I replied, and they left the court room.

"Who were they?" Thor asked.

"Just journalists," I replied.

ABOUT THE AUTHOR

Lisa is married to Rich, has 3 children, 2 granddaughters, and many cats. Born and bred in Leicester, she lived in Kent for 10 years and now resides in Derby.

More books by Lisa:

Why I Have So Many Cats (Poetry)

Winding Down

Searching

Covid-Nineteen Lives

For more information about our books, or to submit a manuscript, please visit

www.green-cat.shop

www.ingramcontent.com/pod-product-compliance
Lightning Source LLC
LaVergne TN
LVHW010055110826
845155LV00028B/354

* 9 7 8 1 9 1 3 7 9 4 0 4 0 *